A Deadly Venture

A Deadly Venture

by Chris Laing

Seraphim
EDITIONS

The publisher gratefully acknowledges the financial assistance of the Canada Council for the Arts and the Ontario Arts Council.

 Canada Council Conseil des Arts
for the Arts du Canada

 **ONTARIO ARTS COUNCIL**
CONSEIL DES ARTS DE L'ONTARIO

Library and Archives Canada Cataloguing in Publication

Laing, Chris, 1936-, author
    A deadly venture / by Chris Laing.

ISBN 978-1-927079-32-4 (pbk.)

    I. Title.

PS8623.A395D42 2014   C813'.6   C2014-905311-8

Editor: George Down
Author Photo: Michèle LaRose
Cover and book design: Julie McNeill, McNeill Design Arts
Inside cover image courtesy of Local History & Archives, Hamilton Public Library

Published in 2014 by
Seraphim Editions
4456 Park Street
Niagara Falls, ON
L2E 2P6

Printed and bound in Canada

To Michèle

"Time after Time"

CHAPTER ONE

FRANK RUSSO WAS ON THE phone, sounding like he had a mouthful of focaccia.

"You'd better repeat that," I said. "But swallow your grub first."

I heard him gulp and he tried again. "We're holding that artist buddy of yours, Roger Bruce, at the Barton Street Jail. And he's asking for you, Max."

"What the hell? Holding him for what?"

"Says he was doing art repairs or some damn thing for a client who's turned up dead. And your boy's the main suspect because it looks like he was the last person who saw him alive. Get over to the station house in five minutes and I'll drive you down to the jail. Fill you in on the way."

"Gotta be some mistake, Frank. I'll leave right away."

I slumped at my desk, stunned ... Roger Bruce? Commit murder? Never.

I lied about leaving right away. Instead, I stared out the window, unfocused for a moment, trying to digest the impossible news of Roger's arrest while I waited for my assistant to arrive for work. The bleat of car horns caught my attention and from my third-floor office I looked down at the early morning traffic – bumper to bumper along King Street, pedestrians bending their heads into a cool October wind, hustling to their jobs at Eaton's, The Right House, the Bank of Commerce; a single-mindedness about them. There was an energetic hum in the air in 1947 as Hamiltonians were anxious to get back to normal after the trials of wartime.

I spotted my legless friend, Bob, setting up to sell his pencils in front of the Capitol Theatre, and he might have been invisible, even wearing his army field cap and his medal, for all the attention the walking tide was paying him. But the war was already old news for many Canadians. Poor old Bob had given his legs and, of course, the rest of his life for his country. But did anyone give a damn?

I sprawled on the office couch and propped up my wounded leg, a souvenir from a beach in Normandy, grateful that I could still walk or, at least, limp. And I was puzzling over why I'd awakened today in such a crappy mood. Maybe it was a premonition, if you believed in that kind of stuff. Maybe a premonition about Roger Bruce.

The office door rattled and I heard my assistant, Isabel O'Brien, chatting with our secretary, Phyllis, as they arrived. I scrambled to my feet and quickly explained Roger's situation. I could read the distress on Isabel's face: we'd gotten to know Roger well during our last case when he helped us identify a painting looted by Nazis and subsequently bought by a Hamilton collector. Since then we'd become good friends with him and I knew Iz was as convinced as I was that Roger Bruce was incapable of committing murder under any circumstances.

I guided her over to the couch and sat her down, holding her hand. "I know it's quite a shock, but see if you can get a hold of Stan Onischuk and have him meet me at the jail." Stan was a defence lawyer who'd recently hired Max Dexter Associates to do investigative work for his firm. "I should know what's happened by the time he arrives."

Detective Sergeant Frank Russo, my boyhood friend, was drumming his fingers on the steering wheel of a dusty black Ford idling at the curb when I limped the short couple of blocks from my office to the station house on King William Street, dead leaves skittering around my feet. I slid in beside him, grateful to be out of the chill fall wind, and he grunted something resembling a greeting. The same as with me, mornings weren't his favourite time of day.

"Listen to that game Saturday night?" he asked me.

"What game?"

"Leafs and Detroit."

"Nah. I hit the sack early. Who won?"

"Nobody," he said. "Two-all tie. They played again Sunday night and Detroit won two-nothing. That young guy from Saskatchewan for the Wings, the one they brought up last year? He's gonna be a helluva player."

"Yeah, I heard about him. Howell or something?"

"Howe. He's a tough bugger – Gordie Howe."

Frank made a left at Ferguson and from there it was just a few minutes' ride down to Barton Street where the high stone pillars and spiked iron fence enclosed the notorious old jail. Frank seemed deep in thought as he hunkered behind the wheel. Was he thinking about my pal Roger behind bars or was his mind still on the hockey game? I just couldn't tell.

"So ... Roger Bruce. What's the story, Frank?"

"Something about restoring a painting, like I said on the phone. I just came on duty, so I don't know all the details but your pal was working at some rich guy's place up by St. Joe's Hospital and according to the housekeeper they had a loud argument. Short time later she discovers her employer's dead body; your artist friend's long gone."

"Did he say anything when he was picked up?"

"Said what they all say: I'm not guilty, Officer. Arrest report says he admitted to arguing with his client – claims he then quit the job, packed up his tools and left in a huff."

Holy Hell! That didn't sound like Roger Bruce and I wondered what had gotten him steamed enough to stomp away from a paying commission.

Frank signed us in at the entrance to the jail while I stood beside him, my first time in this place and I felt the creepy gloom of the dank old building closing in on me. Some folks referred to it as The Barton Street Bastille and I could see why. I'd read in *The Hamilton Spectator* that the family of the jail's Governor lived on the third floor here and I shuddered, trying to imagine their lives. I wondered how they could lead a so-called 'normal' family life in these bleak surroundings. Especially since this was also the place where criminals sentenced to death were hanged and buried. Right here on Barton Street, for Pete's sake.

A guard led us down to the basement holding cells where a sour odour like boiled cabbage hung in the air and he pointed to a makeshift reception room. A few mismatched wooden chairs were pushed against the government-green wall facing an ancient wooden desk in the corner of the room. On the desk a red mantle radio was playing at low volume – one of those nutty novelty tunes, *Open the Door, Richard* – probably a frequent request by the inmates here.

An old guy in a rumpled blue uniform was bent over a desk shuffling papers and pretending not to see us. I noticed a Peller's Brewery calendar thumbtacked to the wall beside him, the previous days x-ed out, and I made a bet with myself that retirement day was on the horizon and couldn't come fast enough.

He finally looked up and said, "Be right with you," as he brushed at the breakfast crumbs decorating his shirt.

"Take your time," Frank told him. "I can see those time sheets must be a helluva lot more urgent than police business."

The old boy did take his sweet time to snap off his radio and set his papers aside, then looked up at Frank with patient blue eyes and spoke in a quiet tone. "Thank you for your understanding, Officer. Now, who do you wish to see and I'll check if he's in?"

Frank clenched his fists, his blood rushing northward to make a ripe tomato of his face as he began to sputter. "The hell do you mean, if he's in? We're here to see Roger Bruce and he'd better be in his goddamn cell."

This guard really had Frank's number, sensing right away how to get his goat by moving in slow motion. He made a production of standing up, replacing his chair just so and turning his papers face down so they wouldn't be read by prying eyes. "One moment please," he said and walked from the room at an exquisitely slow pace.

Frank stomped over to the row of chairs where I'd taken a seat. "You believe that guy? Whatever happened to good old-fashioned common courtesy?"

I tried to stifle my smile. "I thought he was very polite."

Before Frank could wind himself up again, the old guy was back. "Right this way, gents. Mind your step, please."

Along a dark corridor we passed two empty holding cells; Roger Bruce was in the third, hanging against the bars like a shirt on a doorknob, desperation in his eyes. I noticed the bars were covered with a sturdy wire screen, floor to ceiling, maybe so you couldn't pass the prisoner anything he might use as a weapon or to barter for contraband.

The guard nodded toward a vacant cell. "I'll be waiting just over there to take you back upstairs."

Frank grabbed the old guy by the arm. "Just hang on a minute. We want to go in and talk to this man in private."

"No can do, Sergeant. Rules are rules. Police officers investigating a case involving the prisoner can use the interview room upstairs. Same thing for lawyers. Everyone else stays outside the cage down here."

I watched Frank's jaw clenching and unclenching as he glowered at the old guy. "I thought we could make an exception today." He pointed at me. "This man is known to the suspect and can help me with the interview."

The guard shook his head side to side and crossed his arms. "Bend the rules for one then everyone would demand the same treatment. And what's the result?" He glared back at Frank, the benign countenance he displayed before now shot all to hell. "It's anarchy, that's what." Then he shuffled a few feet away to take up his vigil.

Frank almost responded but I elbowed him in the ribs. "C'mon, Bud, he's just yankin' your chain. Forget him, we're here to see Roger."

Frank relented and we turned our attention to the prisoner, who still hung onto the bars so he wouldn't collapse. When he looked up his eyes revealed the battle raging in his head – I could see confusion and anger clashing with his common-sense certainty that this was all a colossal mistake. A pang of compassion zinged through me as I watched my usually easygoing friend now sagging beneath the weight of the justice system.

Roger Bruce was a small-boned skinny guy whose shabby appearance and longish hair belied his Gillette-sharp mind and, according to the artsy set in Hamilton who claimed to know about these things, a growing reputation as an accomplished painter.

I tried to keep my voice upbeat. "Not the happiest day in your life, eh, Pal?"

His eyes showed a tiny spark of life and he forced a grim smile onto his mug. "That's a pretty good guess, Max."

"This is Sergeant Frank Russo, with the Hamilton coppers," I told him. "He's one of my closest friends and he's going to help us sort this out. Why don't you tell us what happened?"

Roger heaved one of those sighs which said, *Here-we-go-again-and-it-won't-make-a-goddamn-bit-of-difference.* He began to shuffle his feet but his pants fell down. "Shit," he said, yanking them up and clutching the waist. "They took my damn belt away so I wouldn't hang myself. Can you believe that? This entire rigamarole is a comedy of errors. And the joke's on me."

Frank observed Roger's frustration in silence and gave him a moment before he spoke in a solicitous tone. "When did you first meet the victim?"

"*Victim?*" Roger's face now red and sweaty. "*I'm* the victim here. Accused of a crime I didn't commit. Let's get our terms straight, Sergeant."

"C'mon, Roger," I said. "I think you're both victims. Now tell us how you met the deceased and what happened."

His shoulders slumped again. "One more time around the mulberry bush, eh Max? I've already repeated my story three times for those other cops and they didn't believe a word I said."

Our eyes locked for a long moment until he realized I wasn't backing off. "Okay," he spoke in a whisper, giving me his whipped-dog look.

Frank and I stood there and waited. Then it all came out in a rush.

"I think I already told you this, Max, but anyway: when I'm short of money, which is often, I do minor repairs to paintings – touch-ups, framing, re-stretching canvases, that kind of thing. I do good work and I'm not too expensive so word's gotten around among the collectors in town. So when my paintings aren't selling I've got something to fall back on.

"Few weeks ago I get a call from a guy named Charles Sherman, a retired businessman, who says he got my name from an art collector friend and would I come by to look at a painting that's in need of repair. We set a date and I went to see him soon after he called. Lives in a big house on Park Street near the corner of Charlton there and he gives me a tour of his large gallery room on the first floor, quite a few nice pieces on display. Upstairs there's a workshop and storage area and that's where he shows me a painting on canvas of Anne Boleyn."

I raised my eyebrows and was about to speak when he cut me off.

"Yes, that Anne Boleyn, one of Henry VIII's wives. He said it was painted by Hans Holbein, a very famous guy, when the artist worked for the king in the 1530s. It was certainly a beautiful piece of work but it had suffered some slight cracking and flaking of the paint, which he wished to have restored. I said I'd examine it and if the repairs weren't too extensive I could give him a price. Otherwise he'd have to seek professional help.

"But right off the bat, I began to doubt the painting was an original. My first thought was: this could be a very rare old painting, so what the hell's it doing here in Hamilton in private hands when any big art museum in the world would pay a fortune for it? So I figured (a) it was stolen or (b) it was a forgery.

"Then I spent a day of research in the library, where I learned that Holbein was known to paint his portraits on wood, not on canvas like this one. I also noted that Anne Boleyn's cloak was painted in what looked to me like Prussian blue with zinc white trim. And neither of those colours was used before the eighteenth century. So I concluded this painting was probably just a copy of the original and reported my opinion to Mr. Sherman the next time we met. I recommended that he take it to the Art Gallery of Toronto where professionals could assess its authenticity."

Frank said, "I guess Mr. Sherman wasn't too thrilled with your opinion, eh?"

"Jeez, that's an understatement. He practically went berserk, stormed around the room cursing me and especially that gallery owner in Toronto where he bought it."

"So what did you do?" I said.

"What could I do? I tried to calm him down. Said I could be wrong, but it wasn't likely. Told him to get another opinion. Or return the painting to where he bought it and have it out with the gallery owner. But he was very upset and not in a mood to listen to me. That's when he demanded I leave. So I bundled up my tools in a hurry and got the hell out of there. Said I'd send him a bill for my time and he chased me out the door."

"In your rush to leave," Frank said, "is it possible that you left one of your tools behind?"

Roger was shaking his head. "Don't think so. I didn't take an inventory or anything but they all seemed to be there. Why?"

Frank shot me a glance which I couldn't decipher then he leaned in closer to Roger. "Because Mr. Sherman's jugular was apparently sliced through with a knife, found at the scene. Looks like your initials on the handle. And, when we check, probably your fingerprints too."

CHAPTER TWO

I HUSTLED UPSTAIRS SEARCHING FOR Stan Onischuk; if anyone was in need of a lawyer, it was Roger Bruce – and right now. I found him cooling his heels in the waiting room on the main floor and we stepped outside to speak in private.

"What's the panic, Max? I'm due in court at ten this morning."

I looked up at Stan; a big guy, well over six feet and a good forty pounds overweight. I knew him from Central Collegiate; not the brightest light in the classroom but a battle tank on the defensive line of the senior football team when the school won the City championship back in '35.

And somehow Stan had managed to come out the other end of Osgoode Hall with a law degree – some said it was good luck while others said it was good connections. In any event, he'd hung up his shingle in Hamilton and was quick to respond when I was canvassing the defence lawyers in town to make a pitch for their pretrial investigative work. So far Max Dexter Associates had worked on two trials for Stan, both of them straightforward fraud cases. Roger Bruce's case, if Stan agreed to take it, was a helluva lot more complicated and could certainly be expensive.

We sat on a bench near the front entrance and I pulled my coat tighter against the wind. Stan took off his suit jacket and stretched his arms across the back of the bench, his ugly-as-hell flowered tie flapping in the breeze. "Great football weather, eh? Tigers are having a shitty season this year, but what do you think of their chances in '48?"

"Not much. Now let's get down to business." I didn't want to waste time gabbing to Stan about his favourite subject so I gave him a bare-bones description of Roger's predicament, ending with the fact that the weapon which had killed Mr. Sherman was apparently Roger's knife.

"Well, hell, Max. It sounds like the cops have a solid case. What makes you think he *didn't* do it?"

"C'mon, Stan. Wrong attitude. Whatever happened to innocent until proven guilty? He admits to having an argument which the housekeeper overheard and he says he must've overlooked his knife as he hurried out of there. He says it must have been found later and used by the real killer."

"Hmm, possible, I guess. Do we know what the police are going to charge him with?"

I shook my head.

"Well, they'll probably do it today and we'll take it from there. If it's first-degree we'll have our work cut out for us. And that'll cost a bit of money, Brother."

"How much?"

"First off, there's bail. That's if we can even get him out on bail. If so, we'll have to post a bond – might cost up to five hundred bucks. And if we go to trial, my fee starts at two grand. More, of course, if the trial is drawn out. It ain't gonna be cheap, my friend."

Actually I wasn't Stan's friend, we were just doing business together. Maybe. I was certain Roger Bruce didn't have that amount of money. Shit, you could buy a brand new Oldsmobile for two grand. Roger's family was well off but I knew he'd rather cut off his right ear than ask them for a dime. Yes, he was a Class A stubborn bugger when it came to making his own way in the world.

I got up from the bench. "Okay, we'll talk it over. Do you want to see Roger now, maybe reassure him that you'll do your best and all that?"

"Sure, Max. I could do that. But the meter starts running as soon as I meet him."

I gave him my hard look. "Jeez, whatever happened to brotherly love? I work for your legal firm, Bud, and I've done the odd favour for you, gratis, free of charge. Couldn't you just go in and hold Roger's hand for two minutes, tell him everything's going to be all right?"

"Of course, I could. But it'll be at my hourly rate and there's a one-hour minimum. What's it to be, yes or no?"

"Hell, no," I said, giving him the consideration he deserved. "And I'll let you know when or *if* we need you."

He got up from the bench, briefcase in hand, ignoring my verbal slap in the chops. "Sure thing, Max. But whichever way you decide it's no skin off my ass."

I watched him saunter away without a backward glance. What a turd! But Roger still needed a lawyer. And *I* certainly couldn't come up with the moolah required: Max Dexter Associates was a new business, just struggling to stay afloat. I'd retained a few accounts from the previous owner but they were small potatoes. That's why I'd gone after some of the city's defence lawyers for pretrial investigative work or anything else they might have. Plus, I had staff salaries to pay: Isabel O'Brien, my new assistant, Phyllis our secretary and her mother, Vera, who worked from her home handling all our credit checks and related info.

As a last resort I could discuss it with my Uncle Scotty, a hotshot reporter with *The Hamilton Spectator*. But that, too, came at a cost, though not in money. I had no doubt Scotty would be acquainted with all the defence lawyers in town and probably some in Toronto as well. And a few of them might even take on Roger's case *pro bono* if Scotty twisted their arms hard enough. However, I'd have him pestering me day and night for details of the case. And, of course, he'd demand exclusive access in order to enhance his position with the *Spec*. He was the only uncle I had but, oh boy, was he a royal pain in the ass.

But we had to act quickly and I wondered … maybe Isabel might have a connection.

I limped back into the Bastille, my knee beginning to throb, and down to Roger's cell where Frank was still chatting with him through the wire mesh.

When they saw me arrive alone they asked, almost in unison, "Where's the lawyer?"

I looked directly into Roger's jittery eyes. "I fired him."

His face puckered in a puzzled squint.

"You kiddin'?" Frank said. "I hate to admit it but your pal here needs one of those bums. And the sooner the better."

I turned to Roger. "Here's the deal. Stan Onischuck is not the man I hoped he was. He won't take a breath without getting paid for it. And I'm guessing your defence fund is whatever you've got in your pockets right now. Which is probably bugger all. So first things first. Can you ask your family to finance your trial if it comes to that?"

Roger's spine became ramrod straight. "No goddamn way. Put that out of your mind right now. I just won't ask them."

I knew he'd say that but I had to ask. Roger's father had insisted that he get a business degree after high school then join the family business. But Roger was intent on attending the Ontario College of Art, which caused a rift within his family. "Okay, leave it with me and I'll see if we can find someone who'll take your case *pro bono*."

I turned to Frank. "Any idea when Roger will be officially charged, and what the charge will be?"

Frank held up his hands like he was fending off an attacker. "Just hold on a damn minute. You guys have to remember I'm the cops. And for now, Roger's the bad guy. So I can't just feed you information out the back door of the station house without getting myself fired. Now, I'll do what I can, when I can, but no promises. You've gotta do this on your own hook."

"Understood, Frank. But what about the timing?" I asked him. "That's sure as hell not a state secret, is it?"

Frank showed me his dark Calabrian scowl but, after a moment's thought, he relented. "Probably today ... maybe tomorrow. Our investigators will meet with the Crown Attorney and make a decision. If it's first-degree murder there won't be any bail unless there are special circumstances, and I don't see any from what I've heard so far. My guess is, if he's charged, Roger would stay here right through the trial." He pointed a finger at me. "That's why he needs a lawyer chop-chop."

CHAPTER THREE

WHEN I RETURNED TO THE office, Isabel was a distressed lioness prowling the room, as agitated as I'd ever seen her. "Tell me everything, Max. What's happening with Roger? This must be a big mistake. What can we do to help him?"

"Hold your horses. Let's sit down – I'll tell you what I know."

We entered my office and I closed the door against Phyllis's tommy-gun typing.

I told Isabel everything I'd learned during our visit with Roger and my unsatisfactory meeting with Stan Onischuck, the money-grubbing creep. "Circumstantial evidence is piling up at Roger's doorstep," I said. "We've gotta find him a new lawyer, PDQ."

"Stan Onischuk was always out for himself. Did you know he's planning to run for City Council in the next election?"

"Nope. But it doesn't surprise me. He's a greedy guy at heart and not all that bright. It was a bum move on my part to solicit his business in the first place."

Isabel had the good grace not to say, "I told you so," and she changed the subject. "I suppose you asked Roger if his family could help him pay for his defence."

"Got the usual tirade. He refuses to ask them. Before I left he even told me not to tell them he's in trouble. I think we've only got two choices: my Uncle Scotty knows all the defence lawyers in town and he could probably talk one of them into taking on Roger's case *pro bono*. But you know what he'd be like – constantly hounding us for details so he could score another big scoop for the *Spectator*."

"And what's the other choice, Max?"

I continued to look at her expectantly, waiting for her to catch my drift.

"Don't tell me it involves me grovelling before that full-of-himself lawyer my father tried to set me up with in the summer. I'd rather slit my wrists."

It was impossible to slide something past her. From the first moment I met her I was convinced that Isabel was a mindreader. She could've had a successful career as a mentalist with Ringling Brothers instead of becoming a Chartered Accountant in her father's firm. And I still counted myself lucky that she'd found the accounting business boring and J.B. O'Brien's old-world views about women too much to take. So it was a happy day last summer when she chucked her position with old Dad and joined Max Dexter Associates to train as a private investigator. And since she was also a CA, well, she was a whiz at managing our business affairs.

"How about this, Max? We'll flip a coin. Heads you try to get Scotty on board and tails I crawl before that arrogant lawyer who's still my father's choice as a son-in-law-in-waiting."

Her red hair flounced on her shoulders and her eyes sparkled with challenge. Was she daring me to allow fate to determine our plan of action? Or was she taunting me about her father's continuing efforts to find her a suitable husband – suitable to him, of course. But maybe her underlying message was that if I didn't get off my ass and express some interest in her, you know, romantically, she might soon be tempted to take up with one of her father's candidates. So perhaps her plan was to stir Yours Truly into action by making me jealous. But maybe that was presumptuous on my part. On second thought, there was probably no "maybe" about it.

My brain became overloaded at this point and I took the easy way out, as I sometimes do. "Okay," I said. "Flip."

I hadn't noticed that she held a quarter at the ready and with a flick of her thumb it twirled through the air landing at my feet. She grinned at me, pointing to the profile of King George VI on the coin. "You won, Max. Heads it is, you lucky dog. I think you should see Scotty right after lunch."

CHAPTER FOUR

THE *HAMILTON SPECTATOR* BUILDING WAS next door to my office on King Street East and I knew it like the back of my hand. During my high school years I spent the summers working at the *Spec*, courtesy of my Uncle Scotty, of course. It was a great place to learn about business and how to get along, or not get along, with a wide variety of people. I spent time in every department during my four summers there: running copy in the editorial department, picking up ads from retail advertising clients downtown, one summer in the circulation department on the truck dropping off the carrier bundles for home delivery as well as supplying the news vendors downtown.

But most interesting to me was the summer I spent doing cleanup and odd jobs for the compositors, typesetters and linotype operators. There were union rules prohibiting me, a non-member, from working directly with the molten lead used in the machines, but a couple of the guys gave me a shot at it after hours.

I still visited there often, usually to see Scotty but sometimes to follow up on past stories in their morgue. I entered the building from King Street and walked past the circulation department where a few customers were complaining about late delivery or missed papers. I nodded at a couple of the old-timers who still remembered me. Past the clamour of the sales clerks in the classified ad section, some of whom were on the phones with customers; others were serving people lined up at the counter. Marie Graziano sent me a big wave and I smiled back. She had taught me some valuable lessons in the newsprint storage cellar.

Near the business office was the elevator to the second floor, which housed the display advertising department as well as the editorial and photographic staff. On the third floor the compositors, proofreaders and page makeup men toiled amid the clatter of their machinery. And even in the elevator I could almost taste the acrid odour of molten lead pervading the vast space up there.

The presses were located in the basement, as was the storage for the giant rolls of newsprint. And you had to wear your ear protectors when those presses roared, pumping out thousands of copies of *The Hamilton Spectator* in several editions every day but Sunday.

I got off the elevator on the second floor and entered the editorial enclave – a sea of desks and newshounds clattering two-fingered at their typewriters; a constant hubbub until that day's issue was put to bed. Reporters were grouped around a horse-shoe of desks where editors shouted to their troops: "O'Flaherty, where the hell's the follow-up to this City Hall story?" "Who was supposed to cover that fire over on Hess Street?"

Past this apparent bedlam I spotted Scotty Lyle in a corner cubicle, promoted to feature writer because of his work on the murder case Isabel and I were involved in during the past summer, not to mention the Evelyn Dick trial stories. Evelyn's murdering and dismembering of her husband John was a helluva way for a man to die, but it didn't hurt Scotty's career a damn bit.

I rapped on the edge of the padded blue divider which marked off his area. "Fancy private space for the famous reporter as he sits with his feet on the desk basking in the glory of his reportorial fame," I said. "What's next, another one of those newspaper awards?"

His feet plopped to the floor and he waved. "Come in, come in." His Scottish burr was still evident thirty years after getting off the boat in Montreal. "I'm always chuffed to see my favourite nephew. How are you, Laddie?"

I ignored his usual line of baloney and sat on the visitor's chair beside his desk. "I need a defence lawyer." I came right out with it, no point in beating around the bush. "Today."

His smile disappeared and he leaned forward. "Go to hell."

"Hey, wait a minute. A few seconds ago I was your favourite nephew. Not to mention the guy who saved your life last summer when you were shot in Niagara Falls."

He glared at me a long moment. "Aye. I forgot about that."

"Bullshit. How could you forget about getting shot in the leg? And being rescued by your favourite nephew? That same nephew who gave you the inside track to write your series on how we solved the Jake Benson murder case?"

I pointed to the walking cane hanging on the coat rack behind his chair. "I saw a lot of guys who suffered from gunshot wounds during the war, Scotty. And most of them would have given anything if all they needed was a cane to get around well enough to go back to their jobs. So I'm sure you'll agree you got a lucky break in that parking garage."

A chagrined look finally appeared on his wrinkly mug. Jeez Louise, sometimes it wore me out helping him to see straight.

"You're right, Max," he said at last. "How can I help?"

"My artist friend, Roger Bruce, needs a lawyer. He's being held in the Barton Street Jail and he'll probably be charged with the death of a wealthy art collector he was working for."

He reached forward, grabbing my arm and said, "Hold on a second." Then he riffled through some papers on the corner of his desk, withdrew a sheet and read aloud. "Charles J. Sherman. Died at his home on Park Street. Knife wounds."

I explained what little I knew about the circumstances but he continued to pump me for details. "You're not listening," I told him. "All I know is what Roger told me and that's not much because he didn't do it. So it's urgent that we find him a lawyer today."

"Tall order, my boy. And these guys are expensive. How much is your friend able to pay?"

"Nothing. We're depending on you to find somebody good who'll take his case *pro bono*."

He gave me his hard look, as though he'd caught me with my hand on his wallet. "Oh, is that all? How did you know I've got a stable of lawyers just chompin' at the bit to offer me free legal services?"

He continued to glare at me but I waited him out. "If by some outside, impossible chance I could find such a lawyer," he finally said, "what would *I* get out of it?"

I was expecting that question: the old Scotty Lyle tit-for-tat ploy for which he held the patent. "First off, you'd get the undying appreciation of Max Dexter Associates."

A Scotty humph.

"And, of course, you'll have access to Isabel or me once a day to update you on the progress of our investigation."

"Once a day," he said, eyebrows raised as though I'd given him a cheque for a million bucks.

"Shouldn't take very long, Scotty. We're very efficient."

He pushed back his chair, reached for his cane and pushed himself upright. "I need a drink. We can limp across the street, eh?"

I followed him out of the building and we crossed King Street at John to the Royal Connaught Hotel, where a corner of the beverage room on the ground floor was reserved as a fledgling Hamilton Press Club.

Two seconds after we were seated a waiter hustled over with a tray of draft beer, dropping off two 10-ounce glasses for each of us. "Forty cents," he said.

Scotty pointed at me. "My rich friend is paying."

I gave the guy a half a buck and told him to have one for himself.

Both of us drained our first beer without pause. Pre-negotiation thirst I guess you'd call it.

"So what do you say, Unc?" I narrowed my eyes at him. "Have we got a deal?"

He drank half his second beer and stifled a burp. "Well, Laddie, it's such a good deal for me I can hardly believe my luck. Just imagine – I get to use one of my hard-earned favours with a certain legal eagle of my acquaintance for your friend the artist who I haven't even met. Bloody Hell, he could be a Mafia shooter for all I know. And in return you or your girl assistant might deign to grant me a few minutes a day to update me on your progress, if any." He drained off the rest of his beer in a long swallow and said, "Who wouldn't jump at a great deal like that?"

Then he raised his arm and signalled the waiter for another round.

Scotty pointed at me when the waiter arrived and I paid again, damnit.

"So what'll it be, Unc? We could both be winners in this deal."

He took a slow sip of his beer and set it down carefully. "No guarantees. But I've got someone in mind who might be agreeable." He reached over and tapped a fat finger against my chest. "But I'll need a helluva lot more than two minutes a day of your precious time."

"Deal," I said, lifting his hand from my chest and shaking it to seal the bargain. I got to my feet and put on my jacket. "Gotta run, Unc. Can you get back to me by the end of the day?"

"I'll try, Laddie. But I've got a sneaking feeling that I'm going to regret this."

CHAPTER FIVE

WHEN I RETURNED TO MY office I tossed my fedora on the filing cabinet beside the door and watched Isabel slowly raise her eyes to mine while she was refilling her fountain pen from a bottle of Sheaffer's Skrip ink. I felt my heart give a little flutter as those green eyes dazzled me.

"Don't distract me, Max. I'm almost done here."

I kept my lip buttoned and signalled with my head for her to join me in my office when she'd finished.

"So how did it go with your uncle?" she said when she entered with one of the big accounting ledgers and plunked it on a side table.

"You know Scotty. It's always wait-and-see time with him. Says he'll think about a suitable lawyer for Roger and let us know soon, maybe today."

"Well, I wouldn't hold my breath. It does seem a lot to ask."

I sent her one of my medium-stern looks. "Not to me, it doesn't. We did save his life, after all, and he still owes us something in return."

"But, Max," she faced me full-on now and those green eyes zapped me. "We certainly didn't help him because we expected a reward or anything."

"No, of course not." I was sputtering, trying to cover up my own need for tit-for-tat. "But he did say he had someone in mind who might be suitable."

My face and neck felt flushed and it made me wonder if I was failing to measure up in Isabel's estimation. Or was that just one of those differences between men and women and I shouldn't worry about it?

"In the meantime," she made a dismissive wave of her hand, letting me off the hook, "there is something else we could be doing until we hear from him. One of the other lawyers you canvassed for work has gotten back to us with a proposal." She went out to her desk and returned with a two-page letter. "It's from the Nelligan and Nelligan law firm, very reputable and a feather in our cap if we sign on with them."

She slid her chair around to my side of the desk and we reviewed the proposal together. "Not bad," I said. "They certainly pay well, but we'd need some extra help to follow up with all these witnesses they want interviewed."

"Yes, and I've been giving that some thought, Max. You remember that nice young man, Trepanier, we met on the Benson case? I recall you were quite impressed with his ability so I wondered if we might borrow him from your friend George Kemper's security company."

What the hell? Trepanier of all people. True, he had the makings of a good detective and his wartime experience with the VanDoos would be an asset. But the main thing I remembered about Trepanier was his suave French accent and the impression he seemed to make upon Isabel. In fact, the bugger had the nerve to ask me if she had a boyfriend. Then he wondered if she would be available for a date. I told him I didn't know about her private life and he'd better ask her himself. And now I was wondering if they'd already gotten together.

I tried to keep my voice light and unconcerned as I asked her, "So ... did you call George Kemper and ask him?"

She sent me a sharp look. "Certainly not, Max. George is your friend and if you think borrowing Trepanier is a good idea then it's up to you to arrange it."

Well, that was about the smoothest passing of the buck I'd ever witnessed. But there it was – sitting in my lap. If I didn't think it was a good idea then I'd risk disappointing her. If I did, then I was opening the door for Trepanier to waltz right in and sweep Isabel off her feet. And on my nickel, goddamnit!

I sat in my chair, eyes downcast, puzzling about how to pass the buck back without getting any of the bad stuff stuck to my fingers.

"Max, are you listening? Maybe you think it's a stupid idea."

"No, no," I was shaking my head. "It's not a bad idea at all. I agree we need the help and Trepanier would certainly be a good candidate. But would he be the best one? Why don't you leave it with me and I'll have a talk with George. Then we can decide tomorrow."

I watched a frown work its way across her brow and imagined her deciding whether I was dismissing her idea out of hand or I really would consider it. "Okay, you're the boss, Max. Meanwhile, I've got some work to finish up on the accounts."

As she walked out of the office, I couldn't stop my eyes from following her. She was wearing a pale grey tailored suit which accentuated her hips with each stride she took, and I had to admit it – she was the classiest woman I'd ever met; the way she moved, the way she spoke, the way she delivered a smile that could melt your heart. And a clean, fresh scent about her like a stroll through the Botanical Gardens on the first day of spring. So, yes, I was probably falling for her. Was I jealous of Trepanier's interest in Isabel a few months ago? Damn right. And was I jealous of her interest in having Trepanier work for us now? Damn right again. But would I do something about it? Damn right – eventually.

It took me a while before I managed to banish these thoughts to the back of my mind, then I began compiling a file for Roger Bruce's case. According to Frank Russo, we'd probably learn of the charges tomorrow, and there were a few notes I could prepare for the new lawyer when Scotty came up with one.

About an hour later, my phone rang and, almost like I willed it to happen, it was Scotty calling to make his report. "I hope this is good news for Roger, Unc. We're counting on you."

"Of course it's good news, Laddie. I said I'd come through and I did. Now just you remember our bargain – I get a complete daily briefing or the deal's off."

"I already agreed to that. No need to go over it again. So tell me, who've you got? And when can we meet with him?"

He paused for a moment and I had an uneasy feeling tiptoeing up my spine. "Scotty?" I said in a loud voice, maybe with a tinge of panic. "Is there a problem? What's going on?"

"No problem, Laddie, you worry too much. I was just think-ing about how fair-minded you are and accepting of people. Because of that I know you'll be very impressed with the law-yer I've found. The name's Rose and I promise you, Max, a real crackerjack."

What did he just say? Fair-minded? Accepting of people? Not like Scotty to flatter me, or anyone else for that matter, so I wondered how big a curveball was coming my way at 95 miles an hour. "When do we meet this Mr. Rose?" I was expecting him to say there'd be a 'slight' delay or the lawyer's out of town right now or some other damn thing which would test my patience.

"Your office at four this afternoon. Now, how's that for ser-vice? You're going to owe me big, Laddie, and I can hardly wait to collect."

At sixteen hundred hours on the nose, Isabel tapped on my door and strode into my office. "We have a special visitor, Max," a mischievous tone in her voice. "She says she knows you."

I looked up from my desk and my heart almost stopped. A Viking goddess sauntered in behind Isabel. She was very tall and slim, a mane of blonde curls haloed her movie-star face. She wore, or rather, was encased in a silvery sheath which fit her firm body like a snake's skin, and she moved with a dancer's grace – a blonde version of Cyd Charisse. Her eyes were locked onto mine and hadn't wavered since she made her slithery entrance. I couldn't tell whether I was having a heart attack or was just short of breath.

Isabel's voice brought me back to reality. "Max, this is Emma Rose, who's agreed to represent Roger Bruce."

Boy, was I wrong when I'd asked Scotty about *Mister* Rose. Iz guided our visitor into the chair beside my desk and made to leave. My head was spinning like a gyro at Emma Rose's appear-ance. The fragrance she wore enveloped me in an exotic cloud and I could see now why Scotty had tried to soften me up for the arrival of this bombshell. He could have warned me! My God, did she look like this every day? I wondered how the judges and other lawyers kept their minds on court business.

"Hang on, Isabel. I think we should talk to Miss Rose together." It was only right that Iz should be included in my meetings, since she now carried half the workload of Max Dexter Associates and Roger was our mutual friend. But more important, this Emma Rose appeared to be the type of woman who might wrap me up like a pretzel and perhaps Isabel could provide, well, a bit of moral support.

"But Miss Rose says she's a friend from school days, Max. So you'd probably prefer to talk in private, catch up on old times." Her voice was as frosty as a brand new icebox and you didn't have to be an ace detective to deduce that Emma Rose's appearance might have something to do with that.

I returned her steely gaze and said, "Well, maybe we could catch up later. But for now why don't you bring up that extra chair and we'll all get to know one another."

We settled ourselves around my desk and Emma Rose, withdrawing an elegant box of Sobranie cocktail cigarettes from her leather briefcase, removed a slim cigarette wrapped in pink paper with a gold foil tip and offered the package to us. Iz and I declined, so she placed the cigarette between her lips and leaned toward me. "Can you ignite me, Mr. Dexter?"

I was nearly mesmerized as I watched her cigarette bobbing up and down while she spoke and I felt a corresponding twitch running up my spine. I had no matches or lighter so I darted my eyes at my assistant and she gave her head a tiny shake.

"'Fraid I can't help you there, Miss Rose."

Reaching into her briefcase again, she came up with a gold Ronson and passed it to me. I fumbled with the mechanism a few times but couldn't get it to fire. She plucked the lighter from my fingers, snapped it alight and directed a stream of acrid smoke toward the ceiling.

There was a bit of a smirk in her deep voice. "You don't remember me, do you, Max?"

I fumbled in my desk drawer to locate the Fischer's Hotel ashtray I kept for smokers, and slid it across my desk toward her. "No, I'm afraid I don't. Please don't take offence though; sometimes I have trouble remembering my own name."

She gave me a sweet smile. "Oh, I remember you just like that. Often saying something was your fault so the other person wouldn't feel embarrassed. You were a good kid and I liked you as much as I liked anyone back then." Emma puffed on her cigarette then stubbed it out and locked her eyes on mine.

I stared back trying to remember where the hell I'd met her. But how could I have forgotten a woman like this?

She read the puzzlement on my face and helped me out. "You were just a Grade 9 kid at Central Collegiate when I was in Grade 11. Don't tell me you've forgotten my so-called legal office I operated out of the girls' washroom on the third floor. You were so embarrassed to rap on the door that you'd left a note, asking me to meet you at that corner store on Victoria Avenue."

I stared at her for a long moment, the memories flooding back in a tidal wave of nostalgia. *Emma Rose*, the tallest girl in the school and rumoured to be one of the smartest. But a gawky, stringbean kid back then whose one-person 'legal' agency defended the rights of the bullied and cheated kids. In my case, she'd discouraged a tough-guy Grade 10 hooligan from 'borrowing' my lunch money whenever he caught me alone after gym period. When I say 'discourage' I mean the guy had his right arm in a cast for six weeks and steered clear of me as though I were one of the school's hated football rivals from Cathedral High.

And here we were again. But now she was an honest-to-God lawyer and probably a lot of other things that I might not like to know about. And I had to admit that whatever else she might be, she had certainly become a luscious Amazon beauty who must have all the heads spinning at the Hamilton Court House.

I stood up and limped around the desk to give Emma a peck on the cheek. "Of course, I remember you now. You saved my life back then, or so it seemed at the time. And I'm really pleased that you've agreed to represent our friend, Roger Bruce."

When I returned to my seat, I asked her, "Did Scotty Lyle have to blackmail you to take this case?"

Emma's laugh was deep and smoky. "Not quite that bad. Let's just say we've come to an arrangement." She gave me a sly wink and lowered her voice to a whisper. "Maybe someday I can tell you about it." Then she reached for her briefcase and withdrew some papers and a legal pad and got down to business. "Now I'd like both of you to tell me what I need to know about Roger Bruce."

Emma Rose left an hour later.

Isabel slumped in her chair and sighed. "I don't mean to sound catty when I say she was a thorough questioner, Max. But Emma could have given those boys in the Inquisition a run for their money."

I smiled at the image of Emma at the Inquisition. "You're right. I was beginning to feel like a barbecued chicken. Let's hope she's just as tough in the courtroom."

She smiled, then fixed me with a thoughtful look. "Well," she drawled the word out and paused for a moment, "appearances are sometime deceiving, aren't they?"

When Emma had stood to leave our office she'd towered over us; I'd bet she was quite a bit more than six feet tall. And I felt Isabel's eyes boring into me as Emma leaned over and gave me a goodbye smooch full on the lips.

"Good to see you again, Max," Emma said. "It's been too long." Then she stretched a sinewy arm toward Isabel and pumped her hand. "Pleasure to meet you too, Miss O'Brien."

I noticed the two women held each others' gaze for a long beat, looking like female versions of David and Goliath, sizing each other up.

Emma glanced toward me, saying, "I'll be in touch after I meet with Roger Bruce and let you know how we might proceed."

And now, Isabel and I were sitting silently in the vacuum left by Emma Rose's departure. I was thinking about our school-time friendship. We'd lost touch years ago and I'd neither seen nor heard about her since. When I glanced at Iz she was deep in thought but I couldn't decipher the introspective look on her face. Was she feeling overwhelmed by Emma's size and swagger? If Isabel had some interest in me, was it too much to hope she could be jealous of Emma's easy way with me? I was never any good at understanding women's subliminal messages. Was any man?

I broke the silence. "We need a plan, Iz."

"You're right. We can't sit around here waiting for Emma Rose to pull some kind of legal rabbit out of a hat. Maybe we should talk with this Mr. Sherman's housekeeper, see if we can get a few more details about his murder than the police were able to."

"Good idea. Then I think we should pay a visit to that dealer in Toronto who sold him the painting. If it's a fake or it's been stolen surely he'd know about it. Unless he's really stupid ... or a crook."

"Maybe both."

I grinned at my assistant. "You're learning fast, Miss O'Brien."

CHAPTER SIX

THE FOLLOWING MORNING WE HAD an early appointment with Grace Clarke, who was employed as a housekeeper for the late Charles Sherman. She'd told Isabel on the phone that Sherman's son lived in Burlington and was the executor of his father's estate. And he was keeping Grace on as housekeeper until he'd decided what to do with the big home on Park Street.

Isabel offered to drive us there and I'd agreed to meet her at oh-eight-hundred at the downtown parking lot she used on Main Street beside the Bus Terminal. I left my apartment on Emerald Street with time to spare and boarded a Belt Line streetcar on King Street heading downtown. I thought I was lucky when I found a copy of yesterday's *Hamilton Spectator* abandoned on an empty seat. I'd just straightened the front page when the woman who took the seat beside me leaned over my shoulder and pointed to the headline. "Isn't it grand," she said, her voice like a fog-horn in my ear, "Prime Minister King will be attending Princess Elizabeth's wedding on November the twentieth. Why, that's less than a month away."

My eyes were smarting from the odour of her high-octane perfume and I was about to give her one of my withering looks, but I toned it down since she appeared to be an old-age pensioner as well as a Nosy Parker. I turned the page only to find a large photo of the Princess and Lieutenant Philip Mountbatten dressed in full regalia. "Such a handsome couple," my seatmate said, reaching over to angle the page in her direction. "It's like a fairy tale come true."

I re-folded the paper and handed it to her. "This is my stop, Madam. Here – take the paper with my compliments."

I found myself at the corner of King Street and Ferguson and my early departure from the streetcar meant that I had to limp several extra blocks before reaching my destination. I never claimed that all my decisions were rational.

Some of the stores along this stretch of King were decked out with Hallowe'en decorations: witches on broomsticks hanging in the windows and an array of scary masks on display. A long table of pumpkins, some of them carved as jack-o-lanterns, attracted a knot of onlookers in front of Carroll's Grocery Store. It brought back a rush of youthful memories, maybe because I hadn't seen this Hallowe'en stuff since heading for England in '39 and the Brits didn't celebrate it as we did.

When I reached the parking lot, I spotted Isabel standing beside her sporty '47 Studebaker coupé watching for me in the direction of our office. I paused a moment to admire her smart appearance; she was wrapped like a Christmas present in a full-length green coat which contrasted with her flaming red hair. She was so focused upon her vigil that I was able to approach her unnoticed. "Trick or treat!" I said, and she snapped around to face me, clutching her oversize handbag, ready to swing it in my direction.

As soon as she recognized me the tension drained from her eyes. "You were lucky, Max."

"I'll say. You could've taken my head off with that satchel you carry."

She gave me that look which women use instead of giving you a kick in the pants. "Very funny," she said. "Now jump in or we'll be late." Her sense of humour wasn't as finely-developed as mine but maybe we had different views on what was funny.

Isabel had joined Max Dexter Associates just a few months ago and, so far, had proved invaluable to the success of my small agency. But from time to time I had the feeling that she was the dog and I was the tail. And I still hadn't decided whether that was a good thing or a bad thing.

We turned off James South at Charlton, made a right on Park Street and stopped in front of the murder victim's house, where two gardeners were raking up curling leaves from under the elms and maples lining the large corner lot.

We were greeted at the front door by a dark-skinned woman, and my stereotypical image from the movies of a Negro housekeeper who smiles and nods and says "Yassuh" clashed with the striking image of Grace Clarke. She wore a fashionable white dress which could have passed for a uniform if it weren't for the wide padded shoulders and the narrow waist cinched with a black belt. Her manner was cool and in charge, almost like the lady of the manor. "Do come in," she said. "I've been expecting you."

We followed her along a thickly carpeted hallway toward the rear of the house, enticed by the aroma of fresh coffee. Isabel raised her eyebrows at me when she caught me admiring the sway of Grace's hips as she glided like a fashion model in a pair of low-heeled black pumps toward a kitchen which looked to be larger than the White Spot Grill. She pointed to a breakfast nook in the corner by a bay window where a young lad was shovelling cereal into his mouth. "Have a seat. Coffee's on the way."

Then she placed her hand on the boy's arm, slowing him down. "Eat like a gentleman, Vincent. We have visitors, after all."

The boy said, "Yes, Mama," but kept up his pace when she removed her hand.

I grinned at him when he snuck a peek at me between bites. A fine-featured boy about ten years of age and slim like his mother. But not quite as dark, his skin the colour of coffee when you were generous with the milk. And a spark in his eye when I smiled and said, "You're making short work of those Shreddies, Bud. You late for school this morning?"

"No, Sir. But I hate soggy Shreddies."

"Me too. And Grape-Nuts are even worse."

Grace brought a tray of coffee cups and a steaming carafe to the table. "It's nice that you boys are getting along, Mr. Dexter. But Vincent has to get ready for school." She took his empty bowl from him. "Go and wash up now. And don't dawdle up there."

"He's a very nice boy, Mrs. Clarke," Isabel said after he'd gone. "You and your husband must be proud of him."

"Thank you, Miss. But sadly, my husband has passed away." She became silent for a moment then added, "He was very proud of his boy." She poured three cups of coffee and passed us the cream and sugar. "I hope this won't take too long. I have an appointment later this morning."

Isabel added some cream and handed it to me. "We won't overstay our welcome. As I mentioned on the phone, we're assisting with the defence of Roger Bruce, who's now in jail while the police investigate Mr. Sherman's death."

Frown lines appeared on Grace's brow as she stirred her coffee. "I've already told the police everything I know about that."

"Well, we were hoping you might have remembered other details since the police were here."

I opened my notebook and placed it on the table. "Was young Vincent home at the time of the incident?"

"No, thank God, he wasn't." Grace shook her head now and pushed her coffee cup aside. "Really, this has been a very difficult time for me. I don't like thinking about it, much less discussing the details."

"We understand that," I told her. "But just imagine Roger Bruce's situation. You probably met him when he was working here for Mr. Sherman and I'd be surprised if you weren't impressed by him. Do you really think he could bring himself to kill anyone?"

She looked directly at me, deep brown eyes holding my gaze. Such a beautiful face – she reminded me of Lena Horne in that movie ... *Stormy Weather.*

"I thought he was a nice young man," she said after a long pause. "And I told the police that. He was polite with me and I was shocked to overhear Mr. Sherman arguing with him during his last visit."

"Were you downstairs at that time?"

"Right here at this table. I was writing a letter to my sister in Jamaica."

"You didn't hear sounds of a struggle, furniture being knocked over, that type of thing?"

"I only heard loud, muffled voices. In an argument. Like I said before."

I glanced over at Isabel, passing her the ball, and she gave me a quick nod. "Grace, I was wondering how long you worked for Mr. Sherman."

She levelled her eyes at my assistant and paused, maybe deciding whether or not to reveal personal information to these strangers. She was about to speak when Vincent entered the room with his schoolbag and approached his mother. His Toronto Maple Leafs jacket hung open and she turned toward him to button it up. "Got everything you need, Honey? Hold still for a second – this button's stuck."

He held out a slip of paper he'd slid from his notebook. "Don't forget to sign for my library card, Mama."

I noticed his book had a hockey card pasted on its front cover. "Syl Apps," I said. "He's your favourite player?"

He gave me a proud smile. "Yes, Sir – 25 goals and 24 assists last season."

"Yep, he's pretty good all right. But what about Teeder Kennedy? He scored even more, didn't he?"

"Yes, Sir. He had 28 goals and 32 assists. But Syl Apps is the captain, so that counts for something."

I laughed out loud. "You got me there, Bud."

His mother signed the slip and returned it to his book. "Let's go," she told him and shooed him toward the door. "Say goodbye to these folks."

When Grace and Vincent left the room Isabel leaned toward me, lowering her voice. "Do you think she'll open up to us, Max? I don't want to push her too hard."

"Just remember that people love to talk about their favourite subject – themselves. You can ask the most personal questions which you and I would never answer. But nine times out of ten they'll tell you. So keep on doing what you're doing; she likes you." We heard the front door close and Grace's footsteps approaching so I lowered my voice. "Just continue as long as she'll let you."

Grace bustled into the kitchen, returned to her seat and breathed a sigh. "Now, where were we?"

"You were going to tell us about Mr. Sherman and how long you've worked for him," Iz said.

Grace looked at her closely then gave her a tight smile. "Yes, I guess I was." She sipped her coffee now, taking her time. "Might as well start at the beginning or you'll keep on with your questions ... I lived with my aunt's family in Toronto when I came from Jamaica in 1936." She breathed a dreamy sigh, as if that were a lifetime ago. "Times were tough back then, jobs were scarce and I was fortunate to be hired as a domestic in the big home in Rosedale where my aunt worked. I stayed there four years, got married and Vincent was born in '38. As it turned out, the house where I worked was owned by one of Mr. Sherman's friends. Then, when Mr. Sherman's wife died, he was looking for a housekeeper. The men came to an agreement and I moved to Hamilton, along with my husband and son, at the beginning of the war."

"So you've been here about six or seven years?" I said.

"That's about right. We moved into the third-floor apartment here in 1940, so ..." Grace did the calculation. "Yes. Seven years."

"You mentioned on the phone that Mr. Sherman's son is the executor of his estate," Isabel said. "Are there other children?"

"Not alive. But there were two sons – the younger one died in that ... Dieppe raid."

Grace's eyes were downcast now and the way she said 'Dieppe raid' made me think it might have a more personal meaning for her.

I softened my tone. "I don't mean to pry but did you lose your husband at Dieppe as well?"

Iz shot me a look as though I might've crossed the line and become too personal, but we waited for Grace to respond.

She fiddled with her empty coffee cup, turning it from side to side in the saucer while she thought her private thoughts. "Yes," she finally said. "Owen was 28 when he signed up. I begged him not to because Vincent was only two at the time but ... he and his best friend went to the Armoury down there on James North and volunteered for service. They were assigned to the RHLI." She paused for a long moment. "Now they're both gone."

We sat quietly; the ticking of a grandfather clock I'd noticed in the hallway sounded like military drumbeats in my ears. And it brought back that black memory of '42 when I was a member of the Canadian Provost Corps assigned to traffic control duties at Dieppe. It occurred to me that I might have seen Grace's husband in the horror of that ill-fated assault. What a disaster – such a waste. I didn't doubt that her husband's last thoughts were about his wife and young son he'd leave behind to fend for themselves. What a helluva way to go.

Isabel and I exchanged a glance; her eyes had welled with sadness hearing about Grace's loss. I looked out at the backyard – the leafless trees, the garden plowed under, a cool wind blowing twigs across the lawn. It reminded me of the English country home converted to a hospital where I'd received treatment for my wounded leg. Memories of that damn war still had the power to overwhelm me. And probably always would.

Grace stood up and her coffee cup rattled in its saucer, breaking the silence. She headed for the sink, saying, "I'll put another pot on. Then we can talk about Mr. Sherman."

When she returned to the table she was more composed. "I'm sorry about your friend in jail," she said.

"I'm afraid it was a case of him being in the wrong place at the wrong time," Isabel said. "You mentioned earlier he was polite with you. Did you have a chance to chat with him?"

Grace nodded. "Not for long. When he arrived here Monday afternoon ... just a minute, today's Wednesday ... so, yes it was Monday. Well, Mr. Sherman was on the phone, so he couldn't meet with him right away. So while he waited, your friend was telling me about his exhibition at the Hamilton Art Gallery. He certainly didn't strike me as the kind of man who was capable of murdering anyone."

"And you were right," I said. "Now, when Mr. Sherman got off the phone, where did they meet?"

"Upstairs. There's a sort of art workroom on the second floor. They were only in there for a short time before I heard them arguing. But at that point the gardeners arrived and I had to go outside to attend to them."

"So you didn't see the artist leave?"

"No, I didn't. I spent about ... oh, 10 or 15 minutes outside showing the men what to do and chatting with them. When I returned the argument had stopped and I got busy in the laundry room downstairs so I don't know what time he left."

A timer bell rang and Grace went to the stove to retrieve the coffee pot. She talked as she poured. "I began to wonder why I didn't hear them talking upstairs. Mr. Sherman had the kind of voice that carried, you see. When I went up to check, I tapped on the workroom door and got no reply. I tried again and there was still no response so I went in."

She fixed her coffee with cream and sugar and remained silent for a time, holding her cup in both hands, sipping slowly. We waited for her to continue.

"It was a terrible shock. I saw him on the floor ... face down. But I knew it was him because he was wearing his favourite brown cardigan – I'd given it to him for Christmas last year. And by his white hair." She took a deep breath, then another. "I saw the blood spattered on the carpet as I approached him. Saw that knife, lying near his head as though the murderer had tossed it at the body, finished with his evil work."

I cleared my throat and made a production of adding more cream to my cup for something to do while that graphic image seared into my brain. Isabel reached for Grace's hand and held it. "How awful for you." After a moment, she asked her, "What happened next? Did you call the police then?"

Grace bobbed her head. "Yes. I closed the door and went downstairs to use the kitchen phone. Two policemen arrived shortly afterward and I took them upstairs. They asked me the same kind of questions you're asking now. Then they called for an ambulance and I waited in the kitchen for Vincent to come home."

"The poor kid. What did you tell him?"

Grace continued to stare into her cup while she spoke. "I told him Mr. Sherman had a heart attack and died. He'll learn soon enough what really happened and we'll talk about it then."

That made sense to me and I hoped I would've handled the situation as Grace had done. "Your son seems fine to me," I told her.

"Well, he's sad that Mr. Sherman died. But he's more concerned about where we're going to go next. And so am I, for that matter."

Isabel gathered our empty cups and took them to the sink, readying to leave.

I said to Grace as she stood up, "You mentioned speaking with the gardeners when they arrived. Were they known to you? Same guys who'd come before?"

She began to nod her head and stopped. "Well, yes and no. The older man has been here often but the younger fellow was new to me. They work for the same landscaping outfit we always use so ..." Grace was frowning then gave me a sharp look. "You're not suggesting the gardeners had something to do with Mr. Sherman's death, are you?"

"I don't know, Grace. You were downstairs in the laundry room when Mr. Sherman was killed, so one or both of them could have been involved, right?"

"I suppose so. But, my goodness, why would they do such a thing? I can't believe it."

Isabel stood beside Grace and spoke softly. "Max is just trying to think of every possibility. And I agree with you that it's unlikely those men had anything to do with it. But it won't hurt to check, will it? I can assure you we're very discreet and you won't be involved in any way."

Grace took in a deep breath and let it out slowly. "Well, I think you'll be wasting your time, but the men work for Mohawk Nursery and Landscaping up on the Mountain." Then she led us down the long hallway toward the front door.

I stopped beside the stairway to the second floor and asked her, "I suppose the police sealed up the workroom when they'd finished?"

"Yes, they had me lock it and they took the only key. Until their investigation was complete, they said."

I'd figured the cops would secure the scene until they'd finished their investigation. But maybe they didn't, and I'd've kicked myself later if I hadn't checked. Then something else occurred to me and I asked Grace, "Before we go, would you mind taking us upstairs? Just to see where the workroom is situated in relation to the staircase and the windows?"

She considered my request for a moment before agreeing. "I don't see why not. Follow me."

CHAPTER SEVEN

THE WIND HAD PICKED UP and we buttoned our coats as we left the Sherman house. A sudden gust whipped my fedora off my head and I had to limp at the double to retrieve it.

Iz was smiling when I got back to the car. "You haven't forgotten how to snag a grounder, eh, Max?"

I shook my head, surprised that she remembered my telling her about my illustrious career as starting pitcher for the Napier Street Cardinals when we played at Victoria Park. "I don't have the blazing speed I had when I was twelve. But I still have some tricky moves."

She chuckled at that as she turned left onto James Street, heading back to the office. Then she got back to business. "What did you think of the layout upstairs at the Sherman house? Could the killer have escaped through that window at the end of the hall?"

"Not likely. There's quite a drop to the ground and I didn't see any scrape marks on the ledge from a ladder or a rope. My guess is he walked downstairs and out the front door."

"So he was just lucky not to be noticed by Grace. Or her son when he returned from school."

"Lucky? … I suppose he was. Grace said she was downstairs in the laundry room so she couldn't have seen anyone leave. And I guess her son hadn't yet returned from school. We don't know if the cops canvassed the neighbours – if they did, one of them might've reported seeing a suspicious person, but I doubt it. A big house like that, there'd be service and delivery people coming and going all the time. He might have just walked away without causing anyone to raise an eyebrow."

"So what's next, Max?"

I didn't like to admit it but I was wondering the same thing. "Rule 4(b) in the Detective's Handbook – figure out who benefits from a crime. And Rule 5(a): When in doubt, ask your associate what she thinks."

We were forced to stop at the corner of Hunter Street because a Mammy's Bread delivery van had collided with a farmer's truck carrying crates of chickens to the market. Both drivers and a cop on patrol were attempting to round up the escaping birds and a group of gawking passersby seemed to be cheering for the chickens.

Isabel waggled her head back and forth. "Now I've seen everything. Only in Hamilton, eh?" She pulled out of our lane, made a U-turn and cut over via Young Street to Catharine to get to the parking lot.

We sat in the car there without speaking for a moment until she turned toward me. "It's a good rule – that 5(a). And here's what your associate thinks – we should stay in touch with Grace because she's an intelligent woman and our questions got her thinking. I'm pretty sure our visit convinced her we could be trusted and I got the feeling she might confide in us again."

She tapped me on the arm. "I also think we should pay a visit to Mr. Sherman Junior. If we're looking for someone who benefits from this crime, he seems like the next step. Maybe we can even talk to him before the police do."

I congratulated myself on hiring Isabel as my assistant. Or was it the other way around? Whatever the case, she was one smart cookie and I was glad to have her aboard.

We left the parking lot, cut through the Bus Terminal to King Street and crossed over to our office beside the *Spectator* building.

Tiny, the elevator operator, made a hurry-up motion toward us as we entered the lobby. "Just took your Uncle Scotty up to your floor, Sarge. He's anxious as a sackful of monkeys. Urgent business, he says."

"Anxious is his middle name," I said.

Tiny nodded to Isabel, touching his forehead. "Good day, Miss." Then he slid the brass gate closed after we'd entered and passed me an envelope. "List of the times when that German guy went up to see the immigration lawyer on the fourth floor."

I slid the envelope into my jacket pocket and thanked him.

Isabel turned toward me and winked. She seemed to get a kick out of the way I employed my veteran contacts whenever I could. But what the hell! The ace detective can't be everywhere at once, can he? And my vet buddies were reliable and always grateful for a few extra bucks.

Down the hall on the third floor, Max Dexter Associates was lettered in black on the frosted glass pane. I was still getting used to seeing my name there and having my own business. So far, I liked it.

"Oh, Max, you're finally here." Phyllis was hanging up the phone as we entered and she lowered her voice. "Your uncle's in your office, pacing back and forth."

Isabel picked up her messages and walked to her desk. "Good luck with Scotty. I think I'll sit this one out."

She was used to my love-hate relationship with Scotty from our last case. Of course, I'd felt badly for him when he'd been shot in the leg back then. But it kept him out of my hair for six weeks, so it wasn't all bad.

I hung up my coat and parked my fedora on the filing cabinet, taking a couple of deep breaths on the way to my office.

"What a pleasant surprise," I said. "Long time no see, Unc."

"Enough of your malarkey, Laddie. Now tell me about Charles Sherman, recently deceased, apparently at the hands of your pal Roger Bruce, according to the coppers."

"We'll see about that. Now that Emma Rose is on the case."

He grinned at that, then stopped his pacing and plunked himself in the visitor's chair by my desk. He tapped his cane on the floor. "Tell me the latest, my boy. I don't have to remind you we have an agreement."

"Of course we do. And first off, I want to thank you for sending Miss Rose our way."

"I hope you don't make the mistake of underestimating her ability. Sure, she looks like a ritzy fashion model, but she's as sharp as a tack. Ran rings around a certain hotshot lawyer from Toronto recently, whose name I won't mention. And she has contacts with some of Hamilton's bigwigs – on both sides of the law."

"I believe you, Unc, and I know we'll get along just fine." I straightened in my chair and leaned closer to him. "Now, I'd like to know what's in the *Spectator* morgue about Sherman."

He shot me a stern look, maybe forgetting I'd spent my teen-age summers at the *Spec* and knew about those files kept on the city's important people; all that info ready and waiting in the event of their deaths. Then he pointed a finger at me. "You first, Laddie."

I knew he'd say that and I grinned at him. "I don't have much. Isabel and I met with Sherman's housekeeper this morning. She has an apartment on the third floor of his house where she lives with her young son. Husband killed at Dieppe. Told us the same story she told the police – heard an argument upstairs when Roger Bruce was meeting with Sherman, then she got busy. A while later she went up to check when she no longer heard any-one. Found Sherman's body, face down in a pool of blood. Called the police."

I finished my little speech and leaned back in my chair as Scotty gave me his withering look . "That's it?" he said. "What the hell, I got the same story from the cops yesterday. You must have something more by now."

"Thanks for your confidence in me, but no, I don't."

We stared at each other for a long moment. He knew damn well that I must have picked up something during our visit and I knew he'd keep mum about anything he'd been able to squeeze out of his contacts.

"Your turn," I said.

He huffed out a long breath before he made his recitation, imitating the tone that I'd just used. "Charles J. Sherman. Age 60. Wife died in '39. Two sons – the younger one killed in action at Dieppe. Thomas, the other son, now single, lives in Burlington. Charles Sherman's father and uncle made their fortunes in the electrical power and distribution business. Charles ran the com-pany for a while after the old boys retired, then sold it before the Depression. Since then he became even richer through his investments and land holdings. And now he's dead."

"That's it?" I said, repeating his words.

"Well, we're not certain who killed him, are we? Or why he was killed. According to what you told me about your friend the artist, they'd argued about some painting that might be a forgery. And Sherman ended up dead *after* he'd left."

"That's true, Unc. And we're planning to contact the gallery in Toronto where the painting was bought, see what we can learn – but it could be a dead end. Or have you already done that?"

He shook his head, causing a dusting of dandruff to snow on his shoulders. "Nope. Sounds like baloney to me; something your pal dreamed up on the spur of the moment. What makes you so sure he's telling you the truth?"

I leaned toward him, locking my eyes on his. "Because I know him. And he's an honest guy. I'd bet my life on it."

We continued to stare at each other before he slapped a hand on my desk and stood up. "Okay, Laddie. I just hope you're right."

I called after him as he stalked toward the door. "Hang on a minute. You said Sherman's son was *now* single. Does that mean he's no longer married?"

He stopped at the doorway, a scowl on his mug. "That's exactly what it means. Married only a year before he divorced. No kids; I checked that too. Now, anything else I can do for you?"

"Yeah. When's the funeral?"

His jowls were filling with air, ready to burst. "Friday morning. Christ's Church Cathedral."

I nodded. "Thanks, Unc. Be sure to keep in touch, eh?"

Ten seconds later I smiled when I heard the chatter of the glass panel as he slammed the office door.

CHAPTER EIGHT

ISABEL PEEKED INTO MY OFFICE after Scotty's stormy departure. "My gosh, Max. What did you say to the poor man?"

I shook my head and grinned. "Don't worry about him. He always huffs and puffs when he doesn't get his way." I got up from my desk and stretched. "How about some lunch?"

"I just called down to Spiro; he's sending something up in ten minutes."

That damn Spiro. He owned the White Spot Grill down the street and wouldn't throw a glass of water on me if I was on fire. But nothing was too good for Isabel. Damn good thing I didn't carry a grudge, at least for very long. As far as I was concerned, Spiro could 'get stuffed', something he once barked at me when I asked him to send some lunch up to my office.

We sat at the long table near the window. Isabel was busy with her sliced chicken on brown, while I was having trouble keeping my meatball sandwich off my shirt and tie. We drank a couple of Cokes to wash it down.

Isabel flipped open her notepad. "I called that art dealer in Toronto, Max. He was very polite on the phone. Said he'd have time to see us tomorrow at two and I agreed." Then she raised her eyebrows in that special way which said, *What do you think of that, Buster?*

Was she beginning to take charge of our office now? I thought about that for a moment – but what did it matter as long as the work got done? I made a note on my calendar. "Two o'clock's good. It'll take us an hour to get there so maybe we could use your car." My pre-war Ford was on its last legs and my bank account was telling me, "Tough titty."

"One more thing, Max. Emma Rose said she'd come by after lunch today. She saw Roger at the jail this morning."

I stood up and helped her clear the crumpled wrappers. "Emma Rose," I sighed. "I can hardly wait."

This time she was a subdued Emma. Plain black business suit, which accentuated her Lana Turner figure, and a white blouse. And on her lapel a bright silver filigreed brooch in the shape of a rose – probably her trademark, I thought. She was one classy babe, all right, whatever she wore. She joined us at the table and set her briefcase on the floor beside her.

"So you saw Roger this morning," I said.

Emma turned her head slowly to face me. "No 'Hello, Emma, how are you today? Isn't it a nice Fall day?'"

I felt my cheeks redden, then I ventured a smile. "You're looking very lawyerish, Miss Rose. But no slinky dress this fine day?" Back to her court.

"Not exactly business attire, was it? I wore that silver lamé number for the luncheon and fashion show at the Connaught. It was sponsored by the Hamilton Businesswomen's Club. A fund-raiser for the Red Cross Society and I didn't want to be late for our meeting so I came as I was."

Damn. Why do women always get the last word?

Isabel got me off the hook. "I thought your gown was the cat's meow. I'll bet you stopped traffic when you walked across King Street."

Emma beamed. "As a matter of fact, it did stop for me." She retrieved a notepad from her briefcase. "Now, I'm on a tight schedule today, so … Roger Bruce. He's having a bad time of it in jail but that's normal for a first-timer. Who'd enjoy that smelly old place? A guard brought him upstairs to a visitor's room where we talked. I made some notes to follow up and I'm hoping we might share the workload. Agree?"

"Isabel and I have discussed that," I said, "and it's fine with us."

Emma Rose related Roger's version of his last meeting with Charles Sherman, which accorded with what he'd told Frank and me. "He only saw Mr. Sherman twice, so he really didn't know the man. And what motive would he have to murder him, especially in that gruesome way?"

A silence settled over us, and I tried to imagine the impossible – Roger, knife in hand, standing over Sherman's body as the man's blood pooled on his workroom floor. No, it was out of the question. I asked Emma, "Have the police laid a charge yet?"

"Second-degree murder. I'll argue for bail but I'm not hopeful. It's a fact that Roger was at the scene, the housekeeper saw him. And he admits it was his knife which was found there, even his initials on the handle."

"I was wondering about that knife," Isabel said. "Why would Roger have his tools with him if he was only reporting the results of his research to Mr. Sherman?"

"It puzzled me too," Emma told her. "Roger says he always takes his tool bag with him when he sees a client because he's often called upon to fix something or other – so he brings it along, just in case. When he saw Mr. Sherman that last time, Roger said he used his knife to lift the backing from the frame on the painting they were discussing. He says he simply overlooked it when Mr. Sherman demanded that he leave. Then someone else must have used it."

Roger's version of events made perfect sense to me because I knew him well and I believed him. But what would a jury think as they listened to a prosecutor's impassioned indictment designed to prove his guilt beyond a reasonable doubt? I'll admit it: I was damn worried for Roger.

"Another thing," Emma said. "When I left the jail I dropped in at the morgue at the Hamilton General. Doc Crandall, the coroner, showed me his report. No surprises there. Mr. Sherman died from loss of blood when his throat was slit with a sharp knife. Dr. Crandall said the knife found at the scene was certainly capable of the job. But one small blessing: it was wiped clean of blood and the police found no fingerprints on it."

Emma sat quietly for a moment, tapping her pen on her notepad before she continued. "We have two other criminal defence lawyers at my firm and I'll be consulting with them on our strategy." She turned to me. "Now, tell me about your investigation so far."

"Sure. Isabel and I met with Grace Clarke this morning." I gave Emma the gist of our meeting and summed up by saying, "She told us she saw Roger when he came to the house and went upstairs to meet with Mr. Sherman. She overhead them arguing, then later went up to the workroom where she found her employer dead. I believe her. And so will a jury."

Isabel said, "Max and I are going to Toronto tomorrow to meet the gallery owner who sold the painting to Mr. Sherman. As you know, Roger believes it's not an original, so we'll be interested in his response."

"Good idea," Emma said. "And what about Mr. Sherman's son? I've seen nothing in writing yet, but I presume he's the beneficiary. So we should be talking with him."

I leaned toward Emma. "Why don't you let Isabel and me make the first contact? He might be more open with us than he'd be with the defence attorney for some guy who's in jail for murdering his father."

"Makes sense, Max, but the sooner the better. At this point, Roger's a sitting duck for one of those sharpshooting Crown Attorneys. And it's our job to get him out of the line of fire."

I liked Emma's spirit and I was convinced that Roger was damn lucky she'd agreed to defend him. I asked her, "Why did you take Roger's case without charge?"

Her eyes seemed to be searching mine and I had the feeling she was reading my intentions in asking such a question. I was flattered when she trusted me enough to respond. "Personal reasons, I guess. One of the conditions of my employment with my law firm is that I be allowed to accept one or two *pro bono* cases a year. So I keep my eyes open for people charged with serious crimes who can't afford a good defence lawyer. In Roger's case, I know he comes from a well-to-do family but he refuses to accept their money on principle. And I understand that. I liked him right away, you know, maybe because he's almost as stubborn as I am."

She leaned back in her chair and a smile twitched her lips. "And I have fond memories of you, Max. From the old days."

That surprised the hell out of me. I covered up by saying, "And you owed my uncle Scotty a favour?"

Her laugh was deep and throaty, like a faraway rumble of thunder. "He knows my weak spot. The cases I accept usually attract a lot of press coverage. It's good for my client, good for my law firm and, last but not least, good for me. As for your uncle, well, we have what you might call a tit-for-tat arrangement."

I laughed along with her as Isabel regarded us both with a raised eyebrow and a shake of her head. "Don't get me started on that," I said. "I know it only too well."

CHAPTER NINE

WHEN EMMA LEFT I CALLED Frank Russo at the cop shop. She'd mentioned that the autopsy on Sherman's body had confirmed what we already knew. But I wondered if the coroner had found anything else which might be useful. The trick, as always, was to get somebody in the know to talk to me.

"What took you so long to call?" Frank asked. "Doc Crandall's report has been on my desk for a couple of hours already. You're slippin', Bud."

I expected an earful of his guff and I was pleased he delivered. That was usually a sign he was in a good mood and might be willing to talk. "Jeez, Frank, I just called to inquire about the state of your health, but if you want to tell me about the coroner's report that's all right, too."

"You're so predictable, Maxie. You know damn well I can't release confidential information to civilians."

A low blow, calling me a civilian, but cops were like that. If you weren't part of the brotherhood, well, you weren't part of the brotherhood. Meaning, you didn't have the right to hear some of the juicy bits of insider police info. But I had five years service with the RCMP before I joined the Military Police for the duration of the war. And, as if to rub my nose in it, both the RCMP and the Hamilton Police had refused to hire me after the war because of my wounded leg. And that's why I always got so pissed when cops referred to me as a 'civilian'.

"So you're gonna force me to wait until I get home to read about the autopsy results in the *Spectator*?"

He remained silent for a moment, maybe considering that he was being a jerk.

"C'mon, Frank. You know damn well I'll keep my trap shut. I already know how Sherman died and when. But I'm in the same boat as you are – trying to find out who killed him. Now, if –"

He cut me off. "Stop right there, Mister. I'm not in that boat. We've got a suspect right now in the Barton Street Jail."

I waited until he finished cackling in my ear. "Pretty funny, Frank. But you could at least tell me about fingerprints, eh? I know the knife was wiped down but there must have been prints somewhere."

"How'd you know that?"

"His lawyer was speaking with the coroner."

"Damn lawyers." He paused a moment and I knew from experience he was deciding how much to tell me. "Well, we're still collecting and eliminating," he said, finally coming across. "But we're not finished with the prints yet ... hang on a minute." I heard him shuffling papers, looking for something. "Okay. We found the usual stuff you'd find in a guy's pockets: some small change, hankie, box of Chiclets. And Sherman carried a leather billfold, 30 bucks in it, no photos, some business cards, and a claim check from a jewellery store. Also a key ring from the Hamilton Golf and Country Club with house key, car key, and so on. We're still processing and you didn't hear this from me."

Well, it was better than nothing, but not a helluva lot. "That claim check, Frank. Where's it from?"

I heard a snort at the other end of the line. "What're you gonna do, zip over to the jeweller's and investigate? Hey, wait a minute. I'll bet this is a bit of your famous gumshoe's method, isn't it? 'No clue too small to follow up and eliminate.'"

I waited him out, letting him have his little chuckle at my expense. "The claim check. Which shop?"

"Forget it. I've already sent a guy over to James Jewellers to check. It's only a watch in for repair."

Maybe it *was* just a watch in for repair. But maybe it was more than that. I knew the place on James North, just past the Lister Block, and I thought I might drop in if Frank didn't have anything better to offer. "So that's it? No note saying the butler did it or whatever?"

"Thank you for your call, Sir. Always a pleasure to chat with a Hamilton taxpayer."

I shrugged into my suit jacket and retrieved my fedora from atop the filing cabinet near Isabel's desk.

"Going out to exercise your leg again?" she asked.

"Yep. Walking over to a jewellery store on James North. Frank told me Mr. Sherman had a claim check in his wallet from this place. But it's probably nothing; we'll see. How about you?"

Her leather briefcase lay open on her desk and she was putting together a bundle of official-looking papers. "Going over to the Federal Building, Max. The folks at the income tax office are just dying to discuss your last year's return. That should be fun."

I rolled my eyes. "Better you than me. If I'm not back by closing I'll see you in the morning."

When I left my building I spotted Bob perched on his dolly in front of the Capitol Theatre, his army field cap set at a jaunty angle. The pencils he sold were arrayed on a small tray and their precise order reminded me of a platoon of guardsmen awaiting inspection.

"How are things in the business world?" I asked him. "I heard that Cloke's and Duncan's have closed their pencil departments since you've set up shop on King Street."

He tilted his head back and gave me a mocking laugh. "You're a funny guy, Max; you oughtta be on the radio."

"I haven't see Aggie lately. She still at the United Cigar Store?" Aggie was Bob's sister who wheeled him in his chair to the usual spots where he sold his pencils. Then she'd help him move onto his dolly, on which he could wheel himself surprising distances for a guy without legs.

"Aggie's doing okay. They like her there 'cause she brings in a lotta repeat customers. And speakin' of customers – have you got anything for me, Max? Keepin' an eye on a suspect or somethin'?"

I grinned at him. He was keeping tabs on a guy for me on our last case and got beaten up for his trouble. "Still eager to tangle with the bad guys, eh?"

"Speakin' of that, Max, I had a little incident last week. You know that beat cop, Latner, patrols around King and James there? Anyway, I was set up with my pencils in front of Renner's Drug Store between the bank and Robinson's. All of a sudden this guy comes runnin' in my direction. Latner's chasin' after him and shouts at me, 'Hey, Bob. Stop that guy, he's a shoplifter.' Well, I roll off my dolly and slide it in front of the guy so it'll cut him off. Worked like a charm 'cause it chopped the bugger down at the ankles and he sprawls on the sidewalk ass over teakettle. Pedestrians all around shoutin' at him. Latner arrives and slaps the cuffs on him."

A big grin spread across his weathered mug. "So – whaddya think of them apples?"

"Jeez, next thing you know you'll be gettin' the Mayor's Medal for bravery."

He was still grinning when I left him, and I was thinking that when courage was being handed out, Bob got a double scoop.

The northerly wind picked up as I limped along King Street. I stopped in front of Kresge's and looked over the array of Hallowe'en stuff crammed into the window display. In the next block, a similar range of orange and black streamers and costumes cluttered the windows at Woolworth's, what we used to call 'the five-and-dime' when I was a kid. I still wasn't used to seeing these seasonal exhibits in store windows and their sheer size was beginning to seem excessive to me now. Especially after five years in Europe during wartime when store owners were happy as hell just to have glass in their display windows, much less a gaudy show of seasonal stuff.

I turned right at the United Cigar Store on the corner of James and headed north. "ONCE IN A LIFETIME SUIT SALE – $44.95" was lettered across two windows at Tip Top Tailors. I needed a new suit but I was hoping I could do a helluva lot better than that – maybe down the street at Irving's.

Seeing those suits in the Tip Top window reminded me of the time last year when I'd just returned to Hamilton. I felt flush with my back pay and some money I'd managed to save. I was walking around downtown, thinking about some new clothes, maybe a whole new wardrobe, and I stopped at Lou Davidson

Men's Wear on King Street beside the Russell Williams restaurant. I admired the beautifully styled suits displayed in the window and I strolled in.

A dapper gent approached me, taking a keen interest in how I was dressed.

"I'm in the market for a new suit," I told him. "And that's a beauty in the window."

He smiled and held my arm, guiding me to the door. "Eaton's is having a sale. First floor."

James Jewellers was next door to Peace's Cigar Store on the street level of the old Masonic Hall. A bell tinkled as I entered and a slim man looked up from his work bench and inquired, "Can I help you?"

I approached the display counter near the cash register where the jeweller now stood and I handed him one of my new business cards. "Yes, I hope so. I'm a private investigator working for the person charged with the murder of Charles Sherman. I understand the police have already spoken with you about it."

The man nodded, giving me a slow once-over, no doubt deciding whether to speak to me or not. Now that my eyes were accustomed to the dim light in his shop, I noticed he was a guy in his twenties, slim and trim, someone who looked after himself. And he appeared to be Japanese.

"A police detective showed me a claim check from my shop," he said. "I don't know if I'm allowed to tell you anything else."

"Yes, I understand your reluctance. Most people are unsure of their rights regarding police information. Especially if they come from a foreign country."

I saw his jaw muscles tighten and he squinted at me – hard. "I was born in British Columbia. But I guess some of you eastern Canadians might call that a foreign country."

Ouch, he got me there and I apologized. But, wait a minute. I remembered reading something about Japanese-Canadians during the war. "How long have you been here in Hamilton, if you don't mind my asking?"

He gave me a patient half-smile and I guessed he'd probably been asked to repeat his story many times. "Came here at the end of the war. My sister had moved to Hamilton earlier and I stayed with her until I got my own place."

"And during the war?"

"My family was labelled as 'enemy aliens' in '42 and we were interned for the rest of the war in an abandoned mining camp in the B.C. interior."

I tried to imagine how that might have felt. I failed. "How are you getting along in Hamilton?"

"Pretty good. Along James Street North, we've got people from all over the world. Including lots of Italians, and some of them were interned as enemy aliens too."

I was quiet a moment, thinking about his situation while he gazed at me steadily. "Jeez, that's quite a story. What's your name, by the way?"

He extended his hand and I shook it. "Jim," he said. "Jim Suyehiro." He looked at the card I'd given him. "And you're Max Dexter."

"That's right. I'm looking for information about Mr. Sherman which might help to explain why he was killed. And who killed him. That claim check from your shop, for example. I understand it was for a watch repair – maybe you could tell me about it."

We stood there for a moment without speaking. I was debating whether this visit had come to a dead end as I awaited his response. I figured he might still be worried about the cops and how much he could tell me.

"It was a wristwatch."

I had the feeling Jim Suyehiro might continue so I kept my lip buttoned and let the silence between us do its work.

"It was a Hamilton watch. A very nice one." He was nodding his head. "Not cheap."

"You mean it was made here in Hamilton?"

A smile crept across his face and I wondered what I'd said wrong. "Hamilton is the brand name of this watch. It's a big American company. Well known for its Railroad Grade watches – very accurate."

I returned his smile. "Well, live and learn, eh? But when you say it wasn't cheap, how much are we talking about – 40 or 50 bucks?"

"That model? Hmm. More like 150 dollars, in that range."

Wowski. One hundred and fifty bucks was about the average monthly wage in Hamilton. But Sherman was a rich guy, after all. And since we seemed to be on a roll here, I tried another question. "Don't suppose I could take a look at this watch – that is, if it's still here?"

"Oh, it's here, all right."

"Well, then … you wouldn't be breaking any laws by showing it to me."

His gaze was steady but he shook his head. "I just wouldn't be comfortable with that. And now that Mr. Sherman has, uh, passed away, I think I should notify his wife that I have her watch."

What the hell? I kept my expression carefully neutral. Grace Clarke told us Sherman's wife had died some years ago. So maybe this watch was for a lady friend and Jim the jeweller assumed it was for his wife. I puzzled over that for a moment. "Was Mr. Sherman's wife with him when he dropped off the watch?"

"No, I've never seen her. But Mr. Sherman has been in here a few times, looking for a gift for a special occasion. His office is just down the street, you see. In the Lister Block. And I sold him the watch we're talking about."

"When was this?"

"Hmm, within the last year or so. Then he brought it in a couple of weeks ago. The crystal was cracked and I replaced it."

I thought about the timing but it didn't seem significant. "So he didn't actually tell you it was for his wife."

"No, he didn't. I guess the inscription made me think it was for his wife."

I raised my eyebrows when he said 'inscription' and Jim's expression seemed to say, "Oh, damnit. I shouldn't have opened my big mouth."

I grinned at him. "Why don't you just bring out the watch and we'll look at it together. I promise I won't touch it."

It didn't take him long to make up his mind. He stepped behind the counter, pulled open a wide drawer and riffled through a batch of small numbered envelopes until he found what he was looking for. "Here we are: Sherman." And he slid a gold ladies' watch out of its envelope and onto a black velvet pad on the counter.

I leaned closer when he turned the watch over and I read the neatly-engraved inscription on the back, *ALL MY LOVE* and the initial *C.*

I didn't know the significance of this watch but I felt in my bones it was an important, honest-to-God clue. I thanked Jim for his help, shook his hand and wished him well. Then I hiked back up James Street with a smile on my face and a spring in my limp.

CHAPTER TEN

BACK AT THE CORNER OF King and James I decided to cut across Gore Park and drop in on Longo, one of my contacts at the Royal Connaught Hotel. I kept my eye on the big cop directing traffic. He was waving his arms like a windmill at a couple of streetcar drivers; one was turning off King onto James, the other heading in the opposite direction. The streetcars jerked and creaked through the turn like a couple of old-time horse cars on their way to the boneyard. After they'd passed, the cop pointed at the group of pedestrians where I stood, urging us to get a move on.

I'd heard about this cop. Frank told me the scuttlebutt was that he kept a bottle of hooch in the call box at the corner by the United Cigar Store. When there was a lull in the traffic he'd go over and lean in close to the box for a snort, looking like he was calling in to the station for something or other. People did the damnedest things, even the cops.

In Gore Park, despite the chill in the air, the old-timers still passed the time by trading war stories and chasing the pigeons away. For many of the old boys here, they had nothing better to do. I didn't see anyone I knew, so I continued on to Hughson Street, where a guy on the corner was watching me as I approached. He was having a smoke, leaning against the entrance to the men's washrooms which were underground here; they reminded me of some of the tube station entrances I'd seen in London during the war. The women's washrooms were on the opposite corner, also underground.

When I reached him I said, "Do you know me?"

He shook his head. "No, but I've often seen you limping through the park and I was curious. I figured you for an army guy, wounded overseas and pounding the streets, lookin' for a job."

"Close. But I've got a job. Were you gonna offer me one?"

He choked on his cigarette as he tried to laugh and puff at the same time. "Hell no, Mister. I'm the washroom attendant here at the Men's. When it's not too busy I climb out of my burrow to treat myself to a little daylight and get a breath of fresh air."

I grinned at him. "Yeah, I guess it gets a little stuffy down there."

"You don't know the half of it, Mister. I've gotta mop the damn floor every hour, sometimes more often than that. I'm surprised we won the war."

"Yeah? Why's that?"

"These Hamilton men? They can't aim worth a damn."

I gave him the laugh he was looking for and pointed toward the women's entrance. "You should apply for a transfer. I bet it would be a lot more interesting."

He flicked his cigarette butt onto the road. "Very funny. That's my wife's job."

I left the park at the corner of John Street where I used the side entrance to the Royal Connaught. I took the elevator to the mezzanine level and kept my eye open for Longo, one of the waiters in the main dining room. I checked my Bulova, wishing I could afford a Hamilton watch, and saw it was 1700 hours. Tables were still being set for dinner and I caught Longo's eye as he came my way carrying a tray of glassware.

"Long time no see," I said.

He set the tray down on a nearby table and shook my hand.

I made a show of counting my fingers afterward. "Yep, they're all there. How's business?"

Longo laughed at my little charade. He was a likeable small-time crook as well as a top-notch waiter in this fancy hotel. He'd helped me in the past by keeping tabs on certain of the hotel's guests. Odd that we'd become friends on this side of the pond, given the fact that I'd arrested him in England for liberating supplies from his regimental stores.

"I'm keeping a low profile, Sarge," he said with a smirk. "We've got a new manager and it's gonna take us a while to teach him 'the Hamilton way'."

I shook my head. "No corner too sharp to cut, eh, Longo?"

He touched my arm, guiding me behind a large pillar and spoke in a whisper, "Maitre d's comin' this way. Keep mum."

When the coast was clear, he turned back to me, "What can I do for you?"

"Charles Sherman, recently deceased – know anything about him?"

His eyebrows came together to form a dark V as he thought about it. "Not very much. But I did recognize him from his picture in the *Spec*. You workin' that case, Sarge?"

"Yep. A friend of mine's been charged with his murder. I wondered if Sherman might've been a regular guest here."

"Well, I wouldn't say regular. We saw him once a month or so. Too bad he's gone, though. He was a good tipper."

"Nobody ever accused you of being the sentimental type, eh?"

"C'mon, Sarge. You served overseas, so you know how the world works. People live, people die, and the rest of us carry on."

Listening to him made me wonder if I'd missed the boat and hadn't learned the ways of the world. Maybe life would be a lot easier if I followed his lead: don't concern yourself with others, just keep your eye on the ball and save your own ass.

"Back to Sherman," I said. "Do you recall who was with him when he came here? A group of people? A special woman maybe?" I was still thinking about that ladies' wristwatch at James Jewellers.

Longo's brow furrowed again as he scratched his head. "Don't remember exactly. I did see him with another guy about his age. Don't forget these were old birds, eh? Maybe 60 or even older. But no babes, nothing like that. Oh, and I saw him once with his son."

"How'd you know it was his son?"

"'Cause I've seen him upstairs in the Circus Roof. I work up there on some shifts and I've served his table a few times; a life-of-the-party kind of guy, always with a group of friends. And when he signed the bill, he mentioned who his father was."

The Circus Roof was the Connaught's popular supper club where people in the chips could drink and dance the night away. I wasn't surprised that Longo had made his way up there where the tips were probably in line with the high price of the entertainment.

"What was he like, this Sherman Junior, a nice guy?"

"His name's Thomas. A good tipper like his old man, so what's not to like about him?"

I laughed out loud. If you wanted to work with Longo you had to take him as he was. "I'm interested in this guy Thomas. Maybe you could keep an eye on him for me."

Longo didn't ask me why and I didn't tell him. He just said, "Deal," and we shook on it.

CHAPTER ELEVEN

When I crossed King Street and returned to the office, I found Isabel still labouring over an accounting ledger. "Sorry," I told her when she looked up. "We can't afford to pay you overtime."

She removed the pencil she'd been clenching between her teeth. "I know that better than you do, Max. We'll be lucky to break even unless we dig up a few more accounts before year end."

Truth was, I had no interest in the accounting side of this business. And I hated making cold calls trying to drum up new customers. That's one of the reasons why I regarded the day Isabel began working with me as one of the luckiest days of my life. It was right up there with being evacuated from that Normandy beach to the hospital in England where I got my life back.

Were there other reasons too? Well, just look at her: smart, stylish and definitely easy on the eyes. What more could a guy ask for? The answer was obvious and once again I kicked myself in the backside – what the hell was I waiting for?

"How long are you going to be working?" I said, sneaking up on what I had in mind.

"Another half an hour or so." She had the ability to raise one eyebrow independently of the other. And now the right one was raised suggestively. "Why? What did you have in mind?"

"Well, maybe a drink at Duffy's, if you'd like to."

Now she raised both her eyebrows. "Sounds like fun, Max. Half an hour."

I grabbed the phone book from Phyllis's desk and entered my office, intending to call Thomas Sherman to see if he'd agree to meet with us. Grace Clarke said he lived in Burlington and I found a listing for a T. Sherman on North Shore Blvd.

A woman answered the phone in a pleasant voice and I asked to speak to Thomas Sherman.

"I'm sorry but he's not here right now. Would you like to leave a message?"

"Is this Mrs. Sherman?"

"No. I'm Mr. Sherman's secretary. May I ask why you're calling?"

I gave her a vague description of the nature of my business, glossing over the fact that I was working for the man accused of killing her employer's father. "So it's important that I speak with him as soon as possible."

"Well, I'm afraid that he's extremely busy this week. His father's funeral is the day after tomorrow and we're still making last-minute arrangements. Just leave me your number and I'll have him contact you next week."

I left my number but I sure as hell didn't intend to wait until next week to see him. And why was his secretary answering his home phone?

Iz entered my office carrying the ledger she'd been working on and stowed it away in the metal cabinet we'd recently acquired. Then she twirled the dial on the combination lock with a flourish. The cabinet was waist-high and constructed of sturdy metal. "You can't be too careful when it comes to protecting your important documents from fire or theft," she'd told me when I'd objected to the cost of the damn thing.

Now she turned to face me. "Ready to go for that drink, Max?"

The after-work regulars in Duffy's Tavern crowded along the bar at the back of the room and I was surprised that Liam the bartender could recognize us through the smoky haze as we entered. But he waved and pointed to a table near the bar.

We skirted the dining area, past the big jukebox from which Dick Haymes was crooning "How are things in Glocca Morra?" and I reached for Liam's outstretched hand when he met us at our table.

"Hi-de-ho, Max. Good to see you. And it sure brightens up this joint when you bring the lovely Isabel with you."

Liam's voice was louder than the noon gun at HMCS *Star* and it alerted a number of the barflies to turn our way in order to ogle the striking redhead he was making such a fuss over.

Isabel gave Liam a sweet smile and he hustled around the table to hold her chair while she sat. "My, what service," she said in a Lauren Bacall drawl. "I'm so parched I think I'll have a Singapore Sling."

I felt like a spectator at a Hollywood screen test. "All right," I said. "Enough of this guff. Gimme a Peller's draft – a big one."

Dick Haymes finished singing and was followed by the Nat King Cole Trio sailing through their version of *Straighten Up and Fly Right* when Liam delivered our drinks. Isabel's eyes widened when he bowed with a flourish and set a Collins glass containing a red concoction in front of her.

"Your Sling, Madame." Then he plunked down my beer in front of me, spilling some on my hand as I reached for it.

Iz took a theatrical sip and gave Liam a hundred-watt grin. "Mmmm," she smacked her lips. "Nectar of the gods, my good man. Do you use the same recipe as Raffles Hotel in Singapore?"

Liam was lapping up her attention like a thirsty puppy. "You bet I do. I start with the gin then add Cherry Heering for its nice red glow. Next, some Cointreau and some Benedictine. And finally, pineapple juice, lime juice and grenadine with a dash of Angostura Bitters."

Some of the guys at the bar were still looking our way and when Liam finished his act they gave him a round of applause as he returned to the bar.

Iz took another sip and winked at me. "Liam's such a sweet man, isn't he?"

'Sweet' wasn't the word I'd use but there's no accounting for taste, is there? Liam was a big bruiser of a guy; he'd saved my bacon more than once when we were kids on Napier Street. And now I relied on him for information about his customers from time to time.

I watched her take another sip of the red stuff, then lean back in her chair.

"Maybe we could talk about our visit to the art gallery in Toronto tomorrow," I began.

She fixed those green eyes on me. "We can talk about that during the drive there, Max. It's a one-hour trip, after all."

She was right about that. Judas Priest, it seemed she was right about everything.

"So what did you really have in mind? Just a drink between friends? Or is there something else on your mind?"

I took a long gulp of my Peller's and set the glass down. "Well … I was thinking … maybe we could get to know each other, you know, a little better." There, I said it. For weeks now, I'd been puzzling over how, or even whether, to raise this subject.

Dimples formed on Isabel's cheeks when she smiled. "You're a sly dog, Max. Sneaking up on a girl with your aw-shucks delivery. I think you already know what my feelings are. But it was *your* idea that co-workers shouldn't be involved romantically. So what's changed?"

That was the question, wasn't it? In fact, nothing had changed; I'd liked her from the first moment she'd entered my office last summer. I was concerned at first that I might become steamrollered by such a competent, take-charge type of woman. But now I was surprised as hell that I didn't mind it a damn bit. I guess you could call me Flat Max; run over by Isabel's style and quick intellect. Boy, what a combo!

"What's changed?" I repeated as I drummed my fingers on the tabletop. "It's hard for me to answer that." I drew in a deep breath and let it out slowly. "I guess I'd have to say, nothing and everything. Nothing because I was attracted to you from the moment we met. And everything because I'm … I'm … I'm tongue-tied, that's what I am."

She was smiling as she reached across the table, placing her hand on mine. "It's okay, Max, just relax. I think I know what you're trying to say and I feel the same way. Do you remember that Tommy Dorsey tune, *The Dipsy Doodle*?"

I thought a moment. "Mmm, one of those novelty numbers?"

"Well, sort of. But it describes how you might feel when you're attracted to someone." She hummed a little of the tune, then sang quietly,

"And if it gets you, it couldn't be worse

The things you say will come out in reverse …

That's the way the dispsy doodle works."

I was shaking my head, smiling as she sang. And, as crazy as it sounds, those words were making sense to me. "Where did you hear that tune? At the Alexandra Ballroom on a Saturday night?"

She was nodding. "Yes, there. And, it was a favourite at the Active Service Canteen."

Her remark reminded me of the canteens and servicemen's clubs I'd visited in England. "I hadn't heard of that canteen here. Tell me about it."

She smiled and rolled her eyes. "Well, it was during the war, of course. I used to go to the Saturday night dances with some of my girlfriends. The Canteen was always short of dance partners for the men. And, my gosh, what a beehive of activity it was. It was just across the street from here, up on the second floor at 20 King Street. It served as a recreation centre for servicemen and also some CWACs; lots of games, good food at the snack bar, reading rooms and writing rooms as well. And all run by volunteers. You'd be surprised at how many servicemen were training here during the war, thousands and thousands of them."

"And they all showed up on a Saturday night to dance to *The Dipsy Doodle* with you?"

She was sipping the last of her drink while I spoke, then quickly removed a handkerchief from her purse and coughed into it. "Don't make me laugh while I'm drinking."

Liam appeared at our table. "You folks seem to be getting along. Another round?"

"Not for me," Isabel said. "But that Singapore Sling was super-duper. Besides, Max wants to take me over to the Circus Roof for a little supper and who-knows-what."

Liam took a small step backward as though he'd been pushed. "Well, ain't that hotsy-totsy. You're a lucky guy, Max."

I was as taken aback as Liam and I couldn't think of a smart-ass response. So I left a few bucks on the table and stood to leave. "We'll see you, Pal."

CHAPTER TWELVE

I WAS IN MY OFFICE the following morning at oh-seven-hundred. My head still ached but my upset stomach was beginning to settle down. And my wounded knee still throbbed like an abscessed tooth. There's a word for it – hangover.

I usually draw the line at a couple of beers, but last night – well, all I can say is the devil made me do it. We went to the Circus Roof at the Connaught where Longo met us at the entrance as though he'd expected us. We ordered the advertised light supper while Neil Golden and his orchestra were setting up and the dancing began.

Isabel said she'd felt so good maybe she'd like another Singapore Sling and why didn't I try one too. It's what the temperance folks called the slippery slope. Well, one thing led to another and when Neil and his boys swung into a jivey arrangement of *The Dipsy Doodle*, there was Yours Truly on the dance floor doing his half-assed version of the Lindy Limp.

My memory is fuzzy after that. I vaguely recall Iz saying she'd leave her car in the parking lot and we'd take a cab home. Longo helped me downstairs and poured me onto the back seat of a taxi, and the last thing I recall was Isabel helping me into bed. Did she take the cab home? Or back to the Connaught to pick up her car? Did she stay with me for a while? Overnight? All good questions. But don't look to me for good answers.

And now I was behind my desk, dressed in a suit and tie, waiting for the old Max to come back to life. I'd found a couple of Alka-Seltzer tablets in my desk drawer and limped down the hall to the washroom for a glass of water. And, man-oh-man, I'm always surprised at how loud those damn little tablets can fizz.

By the time Isabel and Phyllis arrived I was nearly normal, well, almost.

But when Iz bounded into my office her voice sounded like trumpets blaring and I put my hands over my ears.

"Where's that frisky guy I saw on the dance floor last night, Max? You don't look like him at all."

On the other hand, she looked like a million bucks this morning in a tailored linen suit, bright-eyed and full of spunk. It occurred to me that I should apologize for last night, but I really couldn't remember much after the dancing. "I think I might have embarrassed you last night. And I'm sorry I was such a horse's patootie."

She motioned with her hand, waving my apology away. "Not necessary, Max. We had a marvellous time and you overdid it a little. I think it was that third Singapore Sling which did you in."

"I had three of those things? Well, it's a wonder I'm able to move at all."

Isabel drew the visitor's chair close to mine. "Don't feel embarrassed about last night, Max. I know you don't make a habit of drinking too much. I'm just glad we were able to enjoy our evening out."

I inhaled a couple of deep breaths and could feel my muscles relaxing. I wanted to ask her what happened after we'd left the Connaught, but did I really want to know? "I'm relieved," I finally said. "I didn't want to do anything to upset you."

She sent me a dazzling smile and I could feel its voltage zing through me. And it seemed to me her smile had more healing power than the Alka-Seltzer I'd taken earlier.

"Ready for our trip to Toronto?" I said.

"All set. We don't have to leave until eleven or so. I thought we might have lunch there because our meeting's not 'til two. That'll give me time to finish up with the income tax people."

"Good. In the meantime, I've got some phone calls to make."

Phyllis came into my office with a large cup of coffee. "Isabel said you'd need a jolt of White Spot java to recharge your batteries, Boss. She had to go back to the Federal Building and said she wouldn't be long."

I thanked her and watched her return to her desk. Phyllis was a willing worker, trying hard to prove she could measure up in this, her first job. A tall young woman, rivalling the impressive height of Emma Rose. That reminded me to call Emma.

The receptionist at her law firm took a few minutes to return to the phone after saying she'd see if Miss Rose was available. "I'm sorry for the delay, Sir, here she is now."

I could hear the click in my ear as Emma picked up the receiver. "Hi, Max ... how are you?" Her breathing sounded laboured.

"Are you short of breath? I'm flattered that you're so anxious to talk to me."

"Always the wise guy, eh? But yes, I'm panting – we've got a basketball net set up in one corner of our parking lot. It's a good way to burn off your aggression, I'm told."

"Well, I'm sorry to drag you in from your workout. I'm calling about Roger Bruce, of course."

"I figured that, but there's not much to report. I met with the Crown Attorney and he might be open to a charge of manslaughter if we can come up with a good argument. But he's one of those hard-nosed guys who says, 'He wouldn't be in jail if he wasn't guilty.' How about you and Isabel? Did you dig up anything useful?"

"Slow going so far. This afternoon we'll be seeing the gallery owner who sold that painting to Mr. Sherman. And I've got a couple more leads to run down. One of them involves an expensive ladies' wristwatch that Mr. Sherman dropped off for repair."

"Mmm. That sounds interesting. Think he might've had a mystery lover?"

"Remains to be seen. Oh, by the way, I called the jail this morning about visiting hours and I was told only family members and lawyers were permitted. Is that true?"

"That's the rule. Visitors are restricted to the prisoner's immediate family and his lawyer. You probably got in before because Roger hadn't been charged then. So if your name's not on the list, you won't get in."

I thought about her answer for a moment. "I wonder if you could include me as part of the defence team. Think that would be possible?"

"Maybe. It's usually the Crown Attorney who complains about the visitor list becoming too long. But I'll look into it and let you know. In fact, I'm going to see Roger later today. Any messages you want me to deliver?"

"Just reassure him we're doing our best to get him out of there. And if I can't get in to see him then maybe there's something I can get him, if that's allowed."

"Okay, Max. I'll call you later."

I sat in silence for a few moments after I placed the receiver back in its cradle. I could picture Roger pacing in his cell right now, his righteous anger simmering, trying to understand the unfairness of his situation. And, shit, I couldn't even get in to see him without a guard looking on. So we had to get him out of there pronto.

I gave my head a vigorous rub, which usually cleared the cobwebs in my brain. But it wasn't helping much this morning.

I'd promised Isabel that I'd contact my friend, George Kemper, to inquire about borrowing the services of Trepanier. He answered after the first ring. "You were expecting my call, George? Picking up so quickly?"

"No. I was going to call a certain lady. You can imagine my letdown." Then he rumbled out his deep laugh. "What can I do you for, Max? Our regular meeting's not 'til next week."

I explained our need for help with the Nelligan and Nelligan law firm contract to interview witnesses for an upcoming trial. "Trepanier impressed me as a pretty sharp guy who'd do a good job, so I'm hoping you'd agree to loan him for a week or so. Of course, we'd pick up the tab for his salary."

"Dunno about that. He's one of my best guys and I'm not in the habit of renting him out like a piece of equipment."

Damn. And I thought this would be easy. "C'mon, George. It's just a small favour for your good buddy."

We both remained silent for a moment, waiting for the other to give. Then I said, "Did you ever clear up that tax problem you were having?"

"Hell, no. And I'm not making a damn bit of headway on it. You know what dealing with the government's like."

"Well, how about this? You loan us Trepanier and Isabel will look into your tax problem. Deal?"

He knew Iz was a chartered accountant and jumped at my offer like a fox on a field mouse. "Deal. When can I get her?"

"Hold your horses, Bud. She'll call you next week; how's that?"

I began to feel drowsy from last night's escapades, whatever they were, and decided to get some fresh air. But I'd just reached the door to my office when my phone rang.

An angry voice bellowed in my ear. "This is John Bruce calling. I'm Roger's father and I want to know what the hell you think you're doing by taking charge of my son's defence. And on top of that, you didn't even have the common courtesy to inform my wife or me that he was in jail. Go on, speak up. What do you have to say for yourself?"

Yikes. I was glad I didn't get calls like this every day of the week.

"How old is your son, Mr. Bruce?"

"What? Just answer my question."

I took a couple of deep breaths, holding onto my temper. "How old, did you say?"

"He's 29, now for God's sake—"

"Hold it right there. You heard yourself – Roger's 29, a grown man, making a life for himself. And he's chosen to do it without your help, Sir. He's my friend and he's being held for a crime he didn't commit. So he asked for my help, which I'm more than willing to provide. Furthermore, he asked me not to contact you and I'm following his wishes."

"Well, what about his mother? She's worried sick about him."

"I'm sorry for her distress but all I can do is tell Roger about her concern. Then it's up to him if he wishes to contact her."

I listened to him gasping for air and probably getting angrier because he wasn't getting any satisfaction from me. But I wasn't in the business of helping a controlling father to exert his will on his adult son.

I heard him sputtering before he slammed the phone in my ear.

CHAPTER THIRTEEN

ISABEL WAS BEHIND THE WHEEL as we sped along the Queen Elizabeth Way toward Toronto. She looked calm and relaxed as her red Studebaker coupé led the pack of eager drivers in the passing lane.

"We're gonna be early," I reminded her for the second time. "So we could drive along the lakeshore instead of fighting this traffic on the Queen E."

I saw the trace of a smile on her lips. "Not my style, Max. By the time we bumped along through Oakville and Port Credit and Mimico, all those little towns, we could've finished our business and been on our way back home."

I opened my mouth to respond – then closed it. Was I going to convince her to take the scenic route? Could I do a better job behind the wheel? Did it matter a damn if we arrived a bit early? Hell, no to all those questions. So I leaned back, closed my eyes and tried to relax.

"How are we doing for time?" Isabel said. "I must've forgotten to wind my watch."

I pulled back my sleeve and checked. "Not noon yet. We've got lots of time." Which reminded me. "I forgot to tell you about my visit yesterday with that jeweller on James Street. Remember I mentioned the claim check found in Mr. Sherman's wallet?"

"Yes. And I forgot about it too. What was it for?"

"An expensive ladies' wristwatch."

"Aha. Sounds like a clue, Max."

"Ask me about the engraving on the back."

"This is getting better. What did it say?"

"'All my love'. And the initial 'C'."

"So you're thinking Mr. Sherman had a lady friend. And he took her watch in for repair."

"We're on the same track. And I'm also thinking you could talk with Grace Clarke about it. You know, 'just between us girls, did he have any lady friends, blah blah blah?'"

"Good idea, Max. I'll call her when we get back."

We reached the Humber River where the QEW became Lakeshore Road and the traffic slowed as we drove alongside Sunnyside Park. On the lakeside, a few intrepid bathers were on the beach but the Bathing Pavilion was closed for the season. The amusement park and midway were still open but with few customers on a school day.

I asked, "Did you ever come to Sunnyside Park as a kid?"

"I just loved it, Max. My favourite ride was the Derby Racer." I turned toward her and saw her eyes light up. "I rode that merry-go-round until I was dizzy."

"Did you see that article in the *Spec*? The government's considering a Lakeshore Expressway to connect the QEW to downtown Toronto. And that would mean the demolition of the park."

"Oh, that'll never happen. I'll bet you anything the people of Toronto are too smart for that. They'll never vote for some smelly expressway to destroy their beautiful park."

Now we were heading downtown on Queen Street, bumper to bumper, catching every traffic light and waiting for streetcars loading passengers in the centre of the roadway. After several blocks of this stop-and-start manoeuvring, I said, "I think I'll take you up on that bet."

Isabel ignored my remark and pulled into a parking spot across the street from Diana Sweets Restaurant. "When I was a little girl my mother used to take me shopping in Toronto. And this was one of my favourite places for lunch."

A polite hostess showed us to a table by the window and left the menus with us.

"It's a nice comfortable place," I said, putting down the menu. "Kind of old-fashioned and cozy. I think I'll have the meat loaf."

After we'd eaten, I stood in line to pay the bill and noticed another lineup in front of a candy and bakery counter for takeout

purchases. I raised my eyebrows toward my companion and nodded toward the counter.

Back in the car, she placed a takeout bag on the back seat and
its sweet aroma enveloped us. "I just love their gooey cinnamon
buns. I bought two but let's save them for the trip home."

We were early for our meeting at the Wellington Street Art
Gallery, aptly named because of its location on Wellington
Street. Iz found a parking space around the corner on Windsor.

The gallery was quite small, on the street level of a tall apartment building. Several big paintings of who-knows-what were
displayed in the window and I rolled my eyes in Iz's direction.

"Try to keep an open mind, Max. Maybe we'll learn something about abstract art today."

A buzzer sounded as we passed through the doorway and
a dapper young man set down a painting he was hanging and
greeted us.

"I'm Patrick McNeill," he said, extending his hand. "I've
been expecting you."

He was a small, good-looking man, smartly dressed in a tailored charcoal grey suit with a snazzy pink tie. We shook hands
and got the introductions out of the way. "I'm preparing for an
exhibit opening tomorrow night, so the place is in disarray right
now." He led us through an exhibit space where a number of
mostly-white paintings were leaning against the walls, waiting
to be hung.

Isabel bent down on one knee for a closer inspection. "Oh, I
like these. They're so … evocative."

When I looked at them close up, they seemed to be unfin-
ished, as though the artist had painted something in red and blue
then partially covered it over with a coat of white. But I wasn't an
art guy so I kept my lip buttoned.

The gallery owner joined Isabel and held one of the paintings so it caught the light from the window. "It's an intriguing
series. The artist is suggesting the remnants of past events which
are vaguely remembered or obscured by time." He pointed to
a section in the top corner of the painting. "And here, she uses

linear elements as linkages between shapes or intimations of what might be hidden beneath the surface."

Isabel stood up and stepped back a couple of paces, turning her head one way then the other. "Yes, I think I see what you mean." She gave him a wide smile. "They're really quite remarkable."

McNeill removed a business card from his jacket pocket with a flourish and gave it to her. "Call me anytime. This exhibit will be up for two weeks, so the paintings won't be available until then. But I'm in Hamilton frequently so, if you're interested, I'd be happy to deliver whatever you buy."

A pretty slick guy, I thought. He was first and foremost a businessman and art was his product. "I don't wish to interfere with the flow of commerce," I said, "but we're here to discuss another matter."

He bobbed his head, set the painting down and we went through to a small office space where we sat surrounded by more paintings stacked against the walls.

"I was shocked to hear about Mr. Sherman's death. And I'm sure you'll understand that I can't talk about some aspects of a client's affairs, even though he's passed away."

Isabel leaned toward him. "We understand that, Mr. McNeill. But it would be useful to us if you could speak generally about the buying and selling of older paintings – like the one you sold Mr. Sherman."

"Well, I'm not an expert in that field." He waved an arm toward the paintings surrounding us. "As you can see, I specialize in contemporary and abstract art. But I also have a number of older pictures in my personal collection. I mention that because it's the reason I met Mr. Sherman. You see, I have a dealer friend whose trade includes such paintings, even a few by the Old Masters. And he sold me that portrait which I later sold to Mr. Sherman. Now, my friend was very explicit about the provenance of that piece. It was not well documented, so it couldn't be definitely ascribed to a particular painter."

"Excuse me for interrupting," I said, "but why did Mr. Sherman come to you?"

He turned toward me, giving me a keep-your-pants-on look. "I was coming to that. Mr. Sherman was one of my friend's regular clients. And when he learned of the painting I'd bought, he became intrigued by it and came here to see it. We got to talking and he made me a good offer, and I sold it to him. That's what I do for a living. But I was very careful to explain the undocumented nature of the piece."

Isabel again leaned forward in her chair. "And you're sure Mr. Sherman understood that?"

"Absolutely. But let me back up a little. Some collectors buy works of art which are said to be 'in the school of' a particular artist, which means it looks like the artist's work but it can't be proven as such. And the painting I sold to Mr. Sherman, a portrait of Anne Boleyn, may have been in the school of Hans Holbein, meaning it might have been painted by him or one of his students or simply in his style by some other painter. However, at some time in the future, improved research methods may show that this painting was actually done by Holbein."

He paused for a moment and I butted in again. "So it's like a calculated risk. If I buy something 'in the school of' some famous painter for a hundred bucks and sometime later it's proven to be really done by him, then I can re-sell it for a million?"

"That's the idea. And that's one of the reasons why some collectors buy works whose provenance isn't yet established."

I shifted in my chair, careful to avoid knocking into a painting. "Is that something that galleries generally note on their bills of sale?"

"You bet your life it is."

I leaned back in my chair and glanced at my associate. I had the feeling that McNeill was more comfortable talking with her, maybe sensing she was a potential customer, and that was okay with me. After all, I wasn't about to let my ego get in the way of learning all we could from this guy.

Isabel caught my intention and turned toward him. "So Mr. Sherman's bill would bear that caveat?"

He bobbed his head. "It's standard practice."

Isabel jotted something in her notebook and continued. "When I spoke with you on the phone I mentioned our artist friend who was contacted by Mr. Sherman to do a small repair. After he examined the painting he did some research which led him to believe it was painted well after Holbein's death."

McNeill held up his hand. "Hang on now. That'll have to be proven by a competent expert in the field."

Isabel was quick to reassure him. "Yes, of course. But if it's true, then the painting wouldn't be worth nearly as much as one done at the time of Holbein, let alone by Holbein himself. Is that correct?"

McNeill sent her a sharp look, maybe realizing she was much more than just a pretty face. "It is indeed."

Isabel flipped her notebook closed and smiled at him. "Thanks very much for your time, Mr. McNeill."

As we walked toward the door, I turned to him. "By the way, how much did Mr. Sherman pay for the painting?"

He frowned at me. "Sorry, I don't release personal information like that. Let's just say, it was more than I paid for it."

We shook hands at the doorway and he smiled at Isabel. "Don't forget you've got my card. I look forward to hearing from you."

Traffic was heavier along the QEW on our return trip and would have been even slower along the lakeshore. So I didn't suggest that we switch routes. Then I wondered, was I becoming a keener listener to Isabel and therefore anticipating her wishes? Or was I being subtly manipulated toward her way of thinking and acting? I decided not to worry about it because it felt good just to be with her.

Isabel half-turned toward me, keeping one eye on the roadway. "I'm beginning to think that painting is a dead end, Max."

"You might be right. But I keep wondering why Sherman became so angry with Roger's opinion that it wasn't an authentic piece. Do you think he might've intended to sell it to someone as an original and Roger's assessment would spoil his plan?"

I gripped the door handle while she passed a convoy of large trucks.

"Even if that were true, it doesn't explain why he was murdered, or who did it. All we know is that someone entered

Sherman's house, killed him with Roger's knife, then disappeared. And it wasn't Roger."

Isabel's unquestioning defence of Roger got me thinking. What if we were wrong about Roger? Could there be something he wasn't telling us about that painting? Or his relationship with Sherman? I didn't want to say anything to Iz, not yet. I'd have to give this more thought.

CHAPTER FOURTEEN

NEXT MORNING, I TOOK SHELTER from the rain under the awning at Nicastro's Grocery Store on James North. Tables on either side of the store's entrance were overflowing with fresh produce: vegetables on one side and bushels of apples from the Niagara Fruit Belt on the other. A pair of old ladies in black dresses picked through the display of tomatoes, shook their heads and moved on to the eggplant.

Across the street two men in dark suits removed a shiny wooden casket from a Blachford and Wray hearse, placed it on a wheeled trolley, draped it in a black cloth and rolled it into Christ's Church Cathedral. Sherman's funeral service wasn't for another half-hour but I thought I'd turn up early to observe the attendees.

I snugged my raincoat a little tighter against the cool wind sweeping up James Street from Burlington Bay and watched a couple of dozen well-dressed mourners entering the old church, none of whom I recognized. Finally a black Cadillac limousine arrived and the driver held the rear door open for an elegant man dressed in black. I assumed he must be Sherman's son, Thomas. I watched him nod to the driver, unfurl his umbrella and stride toward the church. Then a Veterans taxi squeaked to a halt and Grace Clarke stepped from the cab with her young son, Vincent. She paid the driver, clutched her son's hand and they hurried through the rain into the church.

I was somewhat surprised by the small turnout. But I guessed that after retiring from business, Sherman must have lost contact with his old crowd. Or maybe he was the type who never had many friends.

I limped at the double across the street, removed my wet fedora when I entered the church and stood behind the rear pew, studying the backs of people's heads. It was a brief ceremony; the priest droned a solemn eulogy and before long the casket was being rolled toward the large entry doors with the mourners in procession behind it.

Grace spotted me standing in the shadows and approached me. "I'm surprised to see you here, Mr. Dexter. It's not as though you're a friend of the family."

I shook her hand and gave Vincent a pat on the back. "I'm an interested bystander," I said. "And I feel some sympathy for you and Vincent. I'm sure it hasn't been an easy time for you this week."

She gazed at me steadily, her quizzical look still in place. "You're right. It hasn't been an easy time. And I'm worried about where we'll go from here."

At that moment we were joined by Thomas Sherman. Up close, I could see he was impeccably groomed – hair trimmed just so, his suit right out of Lou Davidson's show window, even a high shine on his shoes, despite the rain. "Do you need a ride to the cemetery?" he asked Grace.

"That's all right. We'll take a taxi."

Thomas brushed away her refusal with a wave of his hand. "Nonsense. There's plenty of room in that big car from the funeral home."

Then he turned to me, hand extended. "You're a friend of Grace's?"

I shook his hand. "We met recently." I cleared my throat and thought about how I should explain my presence here. "I'm sorry for your loss, Sir. My name is Max Dexter and I'm working for Roger Bruce's defence team. Roger's been charged with the death of your father and I'm trying to learn about the circumstances leading up to that unfortunate event. I was hoping to speak with you about it."

He gave me a cool appraisal but didn't seem to be annoyed by my being here. Then he shrugged his shoulders, appearing to dismiss the awkwardness between us. "Well, we all have our jobs to do, Mr. Dexter. But this is hardly the time to discuss it."

He reached into a jacket pocket and passed me a business card. "Why don't you call me next week? I'll speak with you then."

He waited for Grace and Vincent to leave the church then followed behind them to the curb, where they got into the funeral car. I knew from the obit in the *Spectator* that interment was in the cemetery on York Street. But I decided to give it a pass; I didn't think I'd learn anything by standing in the rain watching another body lowered into its final resting place. I'd had my fill of funerals during the war, enough to last me a lifetime.

The rain hadn't let up so I called for a Veterans taxi to take me back to the office. Phyllis looked up from her typewriter when I entered, then came over to help me as I shrugged out of my raincoat.

"Isabel's seeing a prospective client – another law firm that might be interested in using our services. She'll be back before lunch." Then she passed me a pink message slip. "Miss Rose wants you to call her, Max."

I limped into my office and called Emma. I imagined her, sopping wet, shooting baskets in the parking lot again.

"No basketball in the rain," she said in response to my joking remark; then she switched gears. "I'm afraid I struck out with the authorities at the jail. You won't be able to see Roger in the lawyers' visiting room. But as part of his defence team you can see him in the holding cell as you did before. It's the best I could do, Max. They're very strict about their visitors' policy."

"Well, thanks for trying. How was he when you saw him yesterday?"

"Not a happy man ... but you knew that already. I assured him that you and Isabel are hard at work on his behalf and that I am doing everything I can to get him out of that place."

I related the details of our trip to Toronto to meet with the gallery owner. "Turns out the owner bought that painting from another dealer and they both knew its provenance was questionable. Mr. Sherman was given the same information, so his murder may have had nothing to do with the painting. That means we've gotta keep digging."

"I'll keep after the Crown Attorney and call you as soon as I come up with anything. I'm still twisting his arm to drop his opposition to my application for bail."

Shit. Emma Rose wasn't making much headway and neither was I. Meantime, my mind filled with that persistent image of Roger prowling in his cage on Barton Street. And I began thinking about that argument with Sherman which Grace Clarke had overheard. It still bothered me that Roger said he'd reported his suspicion to Sherman that his painting may have been a fake. But Sherman already knew it had a questionable background. So what were they really arguing about? And why would Roger lie to me? The quickest way to find out was to ask the man himself.

A Veterans cab dropped me in front of the Barton Street Jail and I checked in with my favourite guard. He went through his usual rigamarole and 20 minutes later I looked at Roger Bruce through the mesh screen which apparently protected us civilians from the vicious criminals here.

"Any news, Max? I don't know how long I can last in this joint."

"Not yet, Bud. But I have to get something straight about your visit with Mr. Sherman when you had that argument."

He picked up on the serious tone of my voice and he stared at me. "What d'you mean? What about the argument?"

"You said that Sherman became angry because you told him his painting might be a fake. But we visited the gallery owner where he bought it and he'd already told Sherman it was undocumented. And now I need to know why you lied to me."

I watched his jaw tighten; he didn't look me in the eye.

"Speak up, Man. Isabel and I have gone to bat for you. Got you a lawyer and we're interviewing witnesses, running around hell's half acre trying to get you out of here."

He seemed to shrink a couple of inches, sagging into his oversized prison outfit. He finally looked at me. "I'm really sorry, Max. I buggered up and I'm ashamed of myself. I understand your being upset with me, but let me try to explain."

I was still steamed, but nodded at him to go ahead.

"Shit. Where to begin? Well, I've been doing quite a bit of that framing and repair work to pay the bills. Things aren't exactly rosy in the art business these days and I'm always short of cash. Anyway, when I was with Sherman that day in his studio, I was prying the painting away from the frame with my knife to examine it and the knife slipped, ripping a big gash across the top of the picture. Of course, Sherman almost blew a gasket and demanded I pay him what he paid for it. Eight hundred bucks. If I didn't pay him in a week he said he'd go after my family for the money."

Roger stopped speaking, staring down at the floor, his teeth clenched. "Then what?" I asked him.

When he looked up at me his eyes were filmy. "We argued. We shouted. And I guess that's what the housekeeper heard. In the end, I told him I'd have to think about it, see if I could raise the money. So I packed up and got the hell out of there. Then the cops picked me up and here I am."

I shook my head, exasperated with him. "Why the hell didn't you just tell me that?"

"I was afraid you wouldn't understand. I know it sounds stupid now. But I didn't want you and Isabel to lose all respect for me. A guy who couldn't make his own living. Not only that, but a guy who took the easy way out of a jam. I can't afford to replace the painting. I figured with Sherman dead, well, nobody would know anything about how it got cut. I'm afraid I just … lost it. I'm very sorry, Max."

"Roger, how are we supposed to work together if you can't tell me the truth? Why didn't you trust me?"

"I know you're pissed off. You have every right to be. And I wouldn't blame you for taking the lawyer off the case."

A long silence stretched between us. "Aw, Hell," I said. "We're not gonna do that. But, goddamnit, we've gotta trust each other. So pretend we're shaking hands through this screen and I'll get outta here."

CHAPTER FIFTEEN

I SPENT MOST OF THE weekend thinking about Roger's predicament, and I made notes of several possibilities for our investigation. But I have to admit it, I was still a little annoyed with him because he hadn't trusted me with the truth about that argument he had with Mr. Sherman.

Frank invited me for Sunday dinner at his home, after which I'd hoped to cajole him into sharing more info about Roger's case. But his year-old twins were now walking and the conversation never deviated from their latest accomplishments.

Shaking her finger at me as I left, Frank's wife, Angela, had said: "Next time you'd better bring Isabel with you. Frank's told me all about her."

I'd overslept Monday morning and it was already past oh-nine-hundred when I arrived at my office and saw Isabel and Trepanier on the office couch with their heads together. Yikes! That was an eye-opener. They appeared to be reviewing the stack of papers on the coffee table in front of them. When I approached, Trepanier leapt up, hand extended. "Good to see you again, Max."

I shook his hand, not putting too much into it. "Glad to have you aboard. Why don't we all go into my office and talk."

I observed that Iz must have cleared the long table in my office where we now sat to review the work plan. "I am happy you remembered me from the summertime," Trepanier said, still with that French accent which Isabel found so endearing. "But I hope there will be no explosion and fire on this job."

I grinned at him, recalling how shaken he'd been when I'd last seen him. He was working a surveillance job for us on the Mountain when the house he was watching was almost blown to smithereens and he was lucky to escape unhurt. "No promises. But surprises are part of the job. That's what makes it fun."

Isabel was tapping her fingers on a red file folder, impatient with my blather.

"Okay let's get down to work," I said. "I see Isabel has the file for the Nelligan and Nelligan job. Did she explain the interviews and background work we've contracted for?"

He nodded. "Yes, we finished talking about it while we waited for you to arrive."

I gave him a sharp look and noticed Iz raising a hand to cover her smile. "That's swell. So you're ready to hit the bricks?"

He stared at me for a few seconds then turned to Isabel. "Hit the bricks?"

She shook her head and smiled. "He means, are you ready to begin with the job? Sometimes people will say they'll hit the road or hit the bricks, meaning they're ready to get going. You'll learn that Max has some different ways of saying things. Not all of them good."

Trepanier still looked a bit puzzled, but said, "Okay. I think I understand."

I stood up, pushed the chair back to the table and decided that I liked a short meeting. "Anything you need ..." I faltered because I didn't know Trepanier's first name so I asked him.

"It's Robert."

But he pronounced it *Row–bear*. I clapped him on the arm and tried out my half-assed French accent on his name, "Okay, *Ro-bert*. Anything you need, just ask Isabel."

When he reached the door he looked back over his shoulder. "Why don't you just call me Bob?"

I sent him off with my best scowl. This office only had room for one wise guy.

I signalled to Isabel to hang back and closed the door. Then I related my meeting with Roger and his explanation about that damn painting.

She shook her head, a sad look on her face. "I'm sorry he couldn't bring himself to tell us, Max. I hope you've forgiven him."

"Yeah, I have. The dumb bugger."

When Iz left I sat at my desk and with a superhuman force of will I drove the images of Roger Bruce and Trepanier from my mind. As somebody must have said, work is the best remedy for whatever ails you. I riffled through my notebook, deciding where to start.

Several directions were vying for my immediate attention: One, find the owner of that watch at James Jewellers; Two, meet with Thomas Sherman, the executor of his father's estate; and Three, speak with those gardeners who tended Sherman's property. I leaned back in my chair, feet up on my desk, closed my eyes, and was letting my mind do its work when I heard someone enter my office.

"Communing with the spirits, Max?"

I remained in my semi-prone position, eyes still closed. "Noooo," I drew the word out as though I were singing it. "I'm trying to retrieve my memory of us dancing to *The Dipsy Doodle*."

When I straightened in my chair and plopped my feet on the floor Isabel was still grinning. "Too bad you don't remember, Max. I never saw anyone jitterbug quite like that."

The playful spirit between us seemed to ebb away when she waved the Nelligan file in her right hand. "*Robert* will be just fine interviewing these witnesses," she said, pronouncing his name with a French flair. I guessed he was part of the furniture for now and I'd better get used to it.

"Phyllis will take the list home with her so Vera can run the credit checks tomorrow."

Vera was Phyllis's mother, who worked from her home because she was wheelchair bound. She'd been conducting her freelance business for years and worked her phone like a professional bookie.

"Good plan. If there's anything to follow up on I can give you a hand."

She was standing beside my desk now, one hand on her hip. "No, I think I'd like to handle this file on my own."

I looked up at her and smiled. I admire a confident woman who isn't a show-off about it. "I think you can do damn near anything you put your mind to. But I'd like to see that report before it goes back to Nelligan and Nelligan."

Her right eyebrow lifted. "Sure thing, Boss."

When she left my office I returned to my list and, after a moment, decided to meet first with Thomas Sherman. Then Isabel and I could see Grace about that watch. And I'd like to take a look at that upstairs hallway again. After that, maybe we could talk with those gardeners. I'd already telephoned the manager at Mohawk Nursery and Landscaping and learned that his men would be working in the area of the Sherman home for the next couple of weeks.

I dug out Thomas Sherman's card which he'd given me at his father's funeral. No answer at his office so I dialed his home phone and reached his secretary again.

"Yes, he told me you might call. He's busy with his father's lawyer this morning but said he'd be here this afternoon after three o'clock. Then he's got, let me see ... Mr. Tedesco's at five, so sure, can you make it for three-thirty?"

What the hell? Did she say Tedesco? No doubt there were other people with that name in Hamilton. But the one who sprang immediately to mind was Dominic Tedesco, the slick boss of the Hamilton Mob who, according to the RCMP, was expanding his criminal empire by taking over legitimate businesses to launder his cash. Was he doing business with Thomas Sherman – or maybe Sherman's old man?

I wondered how big a risk I'd be taking if I asked her which Tedesco she'd been referring to. What the hell, I thought, nothing ventured and all that. So I said, "Tedesco. Uh, would that be Dominic Tedesco?"

She didn't hesitate at all. "Why, yes, it is. Such a nice man. Do you know him?"

A shudder ran through me before I let my breath out. "Uh ... no. I haven't had the pleasure. So – thank you very much for your help. I'll be there at three-thirty, Miss ... I'm sorry, I didn't catch your name?"

"It's Marjorie. Marjorie Scott. Glad to be of help, Sir."

I replaced the receiver and thanked my lucky stars that Marjorie Scott loved to talk on the phone. And I sat there in a bit of a daze, still reeling from what I'd just heard. Tedesco and the Shermans? Shit in a mitt!

CHAPTER SIXTEEN

I WAS STRETCHING WAY BACK in my chair, as near to horizontal as I could get without sprawling onto the floor. In this position you could trace the fine crack lines in the ceiling plaster with your imagination. And after a bit of practice those lines would lead you to the solution of any problem you were attempting to solve. Sure, it was only a theory. But that's what Einstein said too, and look where it got *him.*

Isabel entered my office and stood above me observing my technique. "I don't want to know, Max, so don't even try to explain it to me."

I held out my arm and leaned forward, lucky as hell that she was there to grab hold of me or I would have catapulted forward onto my desk. I gave her a sheepish grin. "It's an exercise – difficult to explain."

She crossed the room and sat at the long table where she waited for me to join her. "*Monsieur* Trepanier had to assist with a small job back at Kemper's Security Agency, but he'll be back after lunch. He's going to work out well, Max. He interviewed Phyllis and me this morning for practice and he has that certain flair about his manner. *Charmant*, I guess you'd say."

I sat without speaking, looking into her sparkling green eyes and wondering if I'd missed the boat with her. "Did you say *charmant* ?"

"He's going to be with us for a week, Max. So we might as well brush up on our high school French."

I couldn't help smiling; sometimes she seemed to bubble over with enthusiasm. And I regretted having to bring her down to earth.

"Some disturbing news." I scooted my chair a little closer to hers. "I spoke with Thomas Sherman's secretary a few minutes ago and I arranged to meet him this afternoon. When she was checking his schedule she was speaking to herself, you know how people do – 'Let's see, he's busy with Mr. Jones after lunch,' etcetera. So it just slipped out when she said that after my meeting with him, Sherman had another appointment at five o'clock."

Iz was staring at me with her eyebrows raised, waiting for the other shoe to drop.

"With Dominic Tedesco."

Her jaw fell open and she covered her mouth with her hand for a moment. "Oh my goodness, Max. Don't tell me we're tangling with him again."

Tedesco was a shady background figure in our last case, pulling the strings which finally ended with four dead bodies from here to Niagara Falls. "We don't know why they're meeting. Tedesco could be raising funds for the Italian Relief Fund for all we know."

Iz had collected herself and now sat straight-backed and eager. "I remember you telling me how he operated, Max, so he could have his fingers in the Sherman family business to launder some of his money."

I watched her eyes, intense with excitement and maybe fear at the possibility of the Mob's involvement in this case. "We'll have to be careful. Remember your Girl Guide motto."

She took a couple of deep breaths and leaned back in her chair. "Yes, I'll 'be prepared'. What do you think we should do next?"

"I'll have a talk with Thomas Sherman this afternoon when you're busy with Trepanier – or should I say, *Robert*?" I saw her mouth give a little twitch, but she remained silent. "So I'd like you to call Grace Clarke, see if we might meet her this morning. That ladies' wristwatch still puzzles me."

Isabel parked at the curb in front of the Sherman residence on Park Street. Two doors down was a large home set back from the street where a couple of boys were playing ball hockey on the long driveway. One of the kids appeared to be darker-skinned than the other so I figured it must be young Vincent. And I wondered why the boys weren't in school.

When I opened the car door Iz reached across and held the sleeve of my jacket. "Hang on, Max. I think Grace might be more open with me if I met with her alone. Just as you mentioned before, remember? 'Between us girls', as you put it. And I think you might be right."

"Okay." I pointed to the kids down the street. "Looks like Vincent and a pal playing hockey. I'll go down and chat with them. I'll be out here somewhere when you've finished."

I watched her approach the Sherman home, where Grace met her at the front entrance. Then I cranked up the car window; the weather guy on CHML said there was a risk of showers. And who knows, maybe he'd be right for a change.

I limped down the street and, when I drew near, Vincent whooped as he snapped a tennis ball between a pair of empty flowerpots in front of the neighbour's garage door. The other boy slapped his stick on the driveway. "Lucky shot, Vince. But I'm still ahead by two goals."

"Who's that wrist-shot whiz?" I called out.

The other kid was taller than Vincent and stocky. He puffed out his chest, showing off his Montreal Canadiens sweater. "I'm Maurice Richard." Then he pointed to Vincent. "And this guy is Syl Apps."

I laughed at their role-playing, remembering my own childhood hero, Ace Bailey, the Leafs' leading scorer long before these kids were even born.

Vincent seemed to recognize me from my visit with his mother. "Did you bring your stick?" he said.

I shook my head. "I'm afraid my hockey days are over. Now I'm just a spectator." I nodded my head toward Maurice Richard and asked Vincent, "Who's your friend?"

"His name's Howard. Lives right here."

I waved at the kid. "Good to meet you, Howard. How come you guys aren't in school?"

"It's some kind of teachers' meeting or something," Howard said. "We don't care what it is as long as we get the day off."

Sharp kid, I thought. Maybe he *would* grow up to be like Maurice Richard.

The front door opened and a tall woman stepped out, her long blonde hair shaped around her face in that popular style they called the Victory roll. But she was no Betty Grable. "Howard, time to come in and get cleaned up. You don't want to be late for your dentist appointment."

The pouty look on the kid's face said he wouldn't mind missing the appointment altogether. Then he dragged his reluctant feet into his house. Vincent called goodbye after him and Howard lifted a hand.

Vincent picked up the flowerpot goalposts, his hockey stick and ball, and I walked slowly with him back home. "How are you doing in school? Top of the class?"

He grinned at me. "Just in sports. Arithmetic and English and all that are pretty boring."

Then we sat side by side on the front steps of the Sherman house while I waited for Isabel. I paused, then dove in. "It's too bad about Mr. Sherman. Was he a nice man?"

Vincent thought a moment before he answered. "He was pretty old and didn't talk to me much. But he wasn't grumpy or anything."

"I guess it was scary for you when you got home from school that day and saw the police and the ambulance and all that."

He turned to face me, shaking his head. "They weren't here when I got home from school. I was playing hockey down the street."

"Oh." I thought about the timing and it seemed to fit. "Did you see anyone go into your house while you were playing?"

"Yes, I saw a man go in, with sorta long hair. And he had a little bag in his hand – like a suitcase."

So he saw Roger Bruce with his bag of tools. "Did he stay very long?"

As I waited for him to respond I was thinking what a helluva good witness this kid was, more observant than many adults. He said, "I don't think it was very long, but we were playing hockey."

"And did you see him come out?"

"He was hurrying when he left. That's all I remember about him."

"Had you seen him before?"

"Nope."

"You've got a good memory, Vincent. Do you remember anything else from that day?"

He went silent on me and I thought he'd run dry. Or maybe he'd decided not to say too much to someone he didn't know well. I waited him out.

"Maybe I shouldn't be talking to you."

I paused. "Why not?"

"My mom says I shouldn't talk to strangers."

"But you *know* me. And my assistant – you remember, that lady I was with before? She's inside speaking with your mother right now."

"Well ..."

I softened my voice. "You *did* see something else, didn't you?"

He was still holding the tennis ball he'd used as a puck, and began bouncing it on the step in front of us. I didn't rush him. He stopped after a few more bounces and gave me a sidelong glance. "I guess I don't remember anything else."

Shit. I sensed he was on the brink of telling me something important but didn't quite trust me with whatever it was. I moved down a step so we were now face to face. "Where were you exactly when you saw the man leave the house?"

He raised his eyes to mine then back to his ball as though examining it for flaws. "In those big bushes there," and he bobbed his head in the direction of a thick clump of cedars across the street.

"And was Howard with you?"

He continued to examine the tennis ball. "Yeah."

What the hell were they doing? Obviously it was something he wasn't anxious to talk about. "Looks like you might be able to see your front door from those bushes."

"Yep. I was watching for my mother to call me in. I do my homework before supper."

I waited for him to continue. When he didn't, I urged him on. "You were doing something your mother wouldn't approve of, weren't you?"

His eyes met mine for a moment, then he began bouncing his ball again. I caught it on the second bounce and moved closer to him. "Tell me what you were doing, Vincent. I won't say anything to your mother unless you agree."

I read the turmoil in his eyes and felt like a shit for putting him through this. But he may have seen something important, so I swallowed my regret and waited for him to answer.

It came out in a whisper. "We were smoking."

I wanted to smile but forced myself not to. "Where did you get the cigarettes?"

"Howard got them. From his mother's purse. Black Cat cigarettes."

"Was it your first time?"

He nodded. "First time with cigarettes." He paused, then continued. "Last week we made pipes out of hollowed-out chestnuts and we used one of those dry weeds with a hollow stem to suck the smoke out. For tobacco we used dried leaves."

I cringed inside, imagining how his mouth must have felt like a fireball when he drew in that hot smoke. "Didn't taste too good, huh?"

He gave me a tiny grin. "It was awful."

"And how about the cigarettes?"

"Not as hot but they tasted real bad."

I reached toward him and gave him a light punch on the arm. "So I guess you're gonna give up smoking, right?"

"Yeah. I don't understand why so many people do it."

"And what d'you think your mother would say if you told her?"

That seemed to send a shiver through him. "She wouldn't like it, I guess. And she'd be disappointed that I didn't tell her." He raised his eyes to mine, probably wondering if I'd squeal on him.

"I think you should talk to your mother about this, Vincent, but I'm not your parent, so it's up to you to do the right thing."

Then I changed the subject, which took him by surprise. "Did you see anything else when you were in the bushes?"

He took a moment to think about it before nodding his head. "I saw another man go in the house after the man with the bag left."

Whoa, Nelly! My mind began to whirl full tilt. Another man. How long did he stay? Long enough to kill Mr. Sherman? If so, this could be the key to Roger Bruce's cell. It took me a moment, but I forced myself to slow down. I didn't want to push the kid too hard and risk losing him.

"Are you sure about this, Vincent?"

"I'm sure, because I was watching my front door, waiting for my mother to call me in."

"But you didn't tell her you saw another man?"

"No, I couldn't. She'd want to know why I was in the bushes."

"Okay. Was it someone you knew?"

"Well, I think so. It looked like Mr. Sherman's son. He was tall and had dark hair. And all dressed up in a suit, like the kind Mr. Sherman used to wear. But I didn't get a real close look, so maybe I'm wrong. Anyway, he only stayed a few minutes before he left."

I sat there stunned for a moment and took a couple of deep breaths before I found my voice. "And what happened next?"

"The police and the ambulance came and I went right home. I'm sorry I didn't tell anyone. Did I do something wrong?"

I gave the kid my most reassuring smile. "No, Buddy. What you did was perfectly all right."

CHAPTER SEVENTEEN

VINCENT WAS BOUNCING THE TENNIS ball again when I heard the front door open and turned to see Isabel and Grace stepping onto the porch.

"Well, here's Vincent," Isabel said. "No more hockey today?"

"No, Ma'am." We both stood up and joined them.

I shook Grace's hand. "Thanks for agreeing to see us on short notice. Vincent has told me something about the day Mr. Sherman —" I almost said 'was murdered', but I remembered how Grace had explained it to Vincent and I said, "about the day Mr. Sherman had his heart attack."

She gave me a sharp look, which I read as a warning that I'd better be careful if I was going to talk about her son. Vincent was looking at me intently too, worried I might betray him.

"Why don't we go in and sit down for a few minutes?" I suggested. "Vincent can tell us again what he saw that day."

We grouped ourselves around the table in the kitchen as we'd done before. Grace sat beside her son, one arm protectively around his shoulder. Her voice was crisp — sharp. "Go ahead, Vincent. Tell us what you said to Mr. Dexter."

I could see Vincent fidgeting, no doubt worried that he'd spoken out of turn to me. His eyes darted to mine and I felt like I'd betrayed the poor kid. But he soldiered on. "I was playing hockey with Howard at his place." He spoke directly to his mother, repeating what he'd told me, but carefully leaving out the smoking business.

When he finished, Grace took a deep breath and patted him on the back. "Why didn't you tell me this before, Honey? Were you afraid I'd be angry with you?"

"I don't know. I guess I wasn't sure."

Grace turned in her chair and wrapped her other arm around Vincent, clasping him tightly to her breast. "Oh, my baby," she murmured as tears streamed down her cheeks. Then she released her son and kissed him on the forehead. "You're a good boy," she said in a whisper. "Now go upstairs and wash up. I'll be up in a few minutes."

After Vincent left Grace went to the kitchen sink, where she wiped her face with a cloth before resuming her seat. And now she wore a determined look on her smooth dark face. "I believe my son," she said in a firm voice. "I'm sure he saw another man come and go after your artist friend left the house. And, yes, I suppose that man could have been Thomas Sherman, but I didn't see him myself."

I opened my mouth to speak but she held up her hand. "Stop right there. I know you'll want Vincent to tell the police what he saw because it could lead them to another suspect and maybe your friend's release from jail. But I can't put a nine-year-old boy through that kind of ordeal. And you heard him; he said he couldn't be sure it was Thomas."

I tried again to speak, but this time Isabel placed her hand on my arm and leaned toward Grace. "I understand your reluctance to place your son in that position, but please think it over. You don't have to decide right now. Why not sleep on it, see how you feel tomorrow?"

Grace was shaking her head, a mother lion protecting her cub. "No. I don't want Vincent involved. You don't know Thomas Sherman. He's not what he seems to be."

I was watching her closely, her mouth turned down at the corners, her black eyes glaring at Isabel, and I wondered about the relationship between Grace and Thomas. She obviously believed that he was a different person beneath that smooth façade. And, of course, I wondered why. "Did Thomas get along with his father?"

I was shocked to hear the anger in her voice when she scowled at me. "This is not your business, Mr. Dexter. I'm sorry if I sound rude but I'm asking you to leave. Now." She stood up and strode to the front entrance where she waited, stone-faced, holding the door open.

We followed her to the door and Isabel tried to speak, but Grace cut her off by closing the door quickly behind us.

CHAPTER EIGHTEEN

WE SAT IN THE CAR for several minutes before we could speak.

"I'm not sure what happened in there, Max."

"Neither am I. But something must've gone on between Grace and Thomas. Or Thomas and his father. And she might be afraid it'll all come out if Vincent's testimony lifts the lid on that Pandora's box."

"Because Thomas is not what he seems to be, she said."

"Yeah. But what does that mean?"

We sat there puzzling over Grace's astonishing reaction for a couple more minutes. I had been hoping to have another look at the layout of the second floor at Sherman's home but that wasn't in the cards now. I turned to Isabel. "Let's go back to the office."

She drove north on Park Street to Robinson where she turned right. "I'm keeping an eye out for the gardeners," I said. "They're supposed to be working in this neighbourhood. Let's drive around for a bit." The homes in this neck of the woods were so superior to the working-class neighbourhood on Napier Street where I grew up that I continued to be stunned by their grandeur. Many contained a dozen rooms or more and their manicured grounds reminded me of the Royal Botanical Gardens. No wonder the owners needed gardeners to keep the grounds in shape.

I spotted a Mohawk Landscaping truck parked down the block and Isabel pulled up behind it.

I opened the car door and turned back to her. "You're not getting out?"

"No, you go ahead, Max. I need a moment to think about why Grace won't talk to us."

I limped across the grass toward the side yard of a large red-brick two-storey home and approached a couple of gardeners who were spreading mulch over the flower beds. "Sorry to bother you, Men. Mind if ask a few questions?"

The older of the two guys parked his shovel against a wheelbarrow and took a couple of strides toward me. "Depends what ya wanna talk about."

He wasn't belligerent, but not a pushover either. When he removed his work gloves I noticed a large area of scar tissue covering the back of his right hand. I pointed my chin toward his scar. "Looks like you might've seen some action overseas; am I right?"

He begrudged me a small grin. "Who wants to know?"

I slipped a card from my jacket pocket, passed it to him and waited while he studied it.

"Private dick, eh? What're ya after?"

"A week ago were you and your partner working at the Sherman house? Park Street near Charlton?"

"Maybe, maybe not." He shot a grin to his partner and they both laughed.

I smiled at him, deciding to join in their fun, and stepped closer to the guy. "C'mon, Man, how about some co-operation here, one vet to another. Or do I have to beat the shit out of you two?"

The big guy gaped for a moment, glanced at his partner, then broke out in laughter, so hard that he was leaning forward now, hands on his knees, gasping. When he straightened, his face was dripping with sweat. "God, that's a good one. Gimpy bugger like you beatin' the shit outta us." Then he waved me over to a set of steps at the side entrance to the house. "Have a seat. We'll talk about it."

When we sat, he removed a pack of Buckinghams from his shirt pocket and offered me one. I waved him off and he and his partner lit up.

"Okay," he said. "The Sherman house on Park Street. He's one of our regulars. We were up there last week, puttin' the place to bed for the winter. Why d'ya wanna know?"

I leaned forward so I could see them both. "So, Monday afternoon, a week ago today, were you working at the front of the house?"

The big guy turned to his partner who shook his head. "Nah, we'd finished the front by then. Took us all day Monday doin' the back gardens. It's a big place, eh?"

"So you didn't see anyone coming or going at the front door?"

"Listen up, Bud," the bigger guy said, "we ain't got X-ray vision. We were out back. So what're ya askin' us for? Ya think we were involved in that murder? We read all about it in the *Spec* and it said the cops have already got the guy in jail who done it."

I looked him in the eye. "And I'm making inquiries. Working for the guy in jail."

He stared back. "Well, well, then there musta bin some hanky-panky, huh?"

I leaned closer and lowered my voice. "I wouldn't be much of a private dick if I didn't keep that private, would I?"

When I returned to her car, Isabel's brow was furrowed. "What took you so long? I thought they'd answer yes, they saw something or no, they didn't. Were they uncooperative?"

"Not after I threatened them with bodily harm."

Her eyes rolled in a gesture I was now getting used to. "You take some getting used to, Max."

"That's what my first girlfriend said."

She folded her arms and gave me a glare. "The gardeners."

I took a long moment pretending to think about it. "Didn't see nuttin'."

"My gosh, sometimes it's like pulling teeth."

I loved the mock-angry look she sometimes showed me. I was getting used to that, too. "Your turn. Grace and the ladies' wristwatch."

She went quiet, rubbing her hands together as though applying some of that Jergen's lotion she kept in her desk drawer. "She's not a very forthcoming woman, Max. Almost as bad as you are with volunteering information. We talked all around the subject, whose watch it might be, had she seen it before, did Mr. Sherman

104 I Chris Laing

buy it for a lady friend, etcetera. And I just couldn't get a straight answer from her."

"And what's that tell you?"

She shifted in her seat to face me directly and spoke with a proud-of-herself grin, "It's her watch, Max. And don't forget that cardigan Grace said she'd bought him as a Christmas gift."

I smiled at her eager expression. "I agree. But why didn't she come clean about the watch?"

"If she did, it might mean that she and Mr. Sherman were more than just employer-employee and she doesn't want us to know that. And she certainly wouldn't want his son, Thomas, to find out if they were close. If his father was really serious about Grace and wished to marry her, Thomas wouldn't like the possibility of sharing the estate with her, would he? After all, he might say, she's only a lowly housekeeper with a nine-year-old son. And just look at the colour of her skin."

"So what d'you think Thomas would have done if he found out that his father and Grace were an item?"

"Well ..." she frowned and her mouth puckered as she thought about it. "I really don't know, Max. So far, nobody's mentioned that Thomas and his father didn't get along. So it's not likely he would have killed his own father, is it?"

It didn't surprise me that Isabel was so incredulous about violent acts committed between family members. Like most law-abiding citizens, she believed that most families would behave more or less like her own, where disputes were usually settled by discussion and compromise. But during my five years with the RCMP before the war, I'd seen my share of those dreaded "domestic" calls when you discovered the bloody aftermath of a deranged father or, on occasion, even a mother.

I pushed those memories from my mind and returned to the present. "But we don't have a better theory, do we? Either Vincent saw Thomas enter the house or it was someone who looked like him. When I see Thomas this afternoon, maybe I should ask him if he did it."

CHAPTER NINETEEN

THAT AFTERNOON I WAS MEETING with George Kemper at his office. He operated Wentworth Security Services out on Beach Road near the Dofasco plant and was a former RCMP instructor I'd met as a recruit. We became reacquainted when he retired to Hamilton and established his own security company. I met with George every couple of weeks to exchange info and shoot the breeze.

When we'd finished up, I called Lefty, the day shift dispatcher at Veterans Cabs. "Well, well, if it ain't Max. How's it hangin', Pal? Haven't heard from you lately."

"Got a new assistant – with a car."

"Yeah, but the car can't drive to two places at the same time, right?"

"Jeez, Lefty, you're smarter than you look. What time's Dave off duty?" Dave was one of my Army buddies who got a kick out of driving me around town when he was off duty. He always refused payment, so every once in a while I'd slip him a couple of flat fifties of Player's cigarettes or a bottle of Canadian Club whisky.

I heard Lefty rustling some papers. "Hang on ... he's finished after he drops off a couple of nursing students at St. Joe's residence. Want him to pick you up then?"

I was standing outside George's office when I spotted a Veterans Cab moving slowly down the street. Figuring it was Dave looking for this address, I waved.

He pulled up in front of me and leaned across to the passenger side to open the door. "How you doin', Sarge? We ain't seen you lately."

"New assistant with a new car. So I'm not givin' you as much business."

"Don't worry about it. Guess you're on a case now and need a lift, eh?"

"Meeting a guy in Burlington at fifteen-thirty but I thought we might drive around out there. Get the lay of the land. Then maybe you could wait for me."

"Sure thing." He flipped his cigarette butt out the window. "Since we've got a bit of time, I think I'll take the scenic route across the Beach Strip. Okay with you?"

"Yep. I don't mind." If I were driving myself to Burlington during business hours I wouldn't take this route. I'd have driven out York Street and along Plains Road. But Dave had a reputation as one of the more aggressive car jockeys in the taxi fleet and he could handle the heavy traffic a helluva lot easier than I could.

We slowed right down at the end of Burlington Street where it merged with the Queen Elizabeth Way because it narrowed from four lanes down to two in order to cross the two-lane bridge over the canal.

Dave muscled his way into the proper lane, ignoring the irate drivers shaking their fists and blasting their horns. Then we joined the snaky line of impatient drivers inching its way along this five-mile sandy strip of land between Lake Ontario on the east side and Burlington Bay on the west. It took us a half-hour to crawl past the summer cottages and year-round homes where Hamilton and area people had lived for more than a hundred years.

We were idling near the busy Dynes Hotel, a popular spot for dining, dancing and drinking which had been here so long the locals joked that Champlain had stayed there on his first voyage to the new world.

Dave glanced at the old hotel. "Jeez, you remember the Dynes, eh, Sarge?"

"Yep."

"Was in a poker game there one night, this was before the war, and we got raided by the cops. Something about bootlegged booze and after hours, you know what I mean. Boy, what a helluva night. I got free room and board at the Barton Street hoosegow for a coupla days."

Just past the Dynes was a large home, now a restaurant, where the Hamilton Police had raided a bootlegging operation during Prohibition and my father was shot and killed by one of Rocco Perri's thugs. My father was a Hamilton cop.

"Hey, you okay?" Dave said.

"Yeah, just daydreaming."

We were approaching the canal now and you could see the bascule bridge above the trees which bordered the road. A small amusement park on the bay side of the road with rides and food stands was mostly closed for the season. On the lakeside was a row of restaurants, some of them open year-round. The traffic was so slow that some passengers could grab a coffee and dough-nut and still catch up with their rides.

"Damn good thing the bridge ain't up or we'd be here forev-er," Dave said. Then he stuck his head out the window surveying the situation ahead. He turned back to me and shrugged. "Well, it was my idea to come this way."

We finally bumped onto the old bridge crossing the canal, a canal which allowed large freighters access to Burlington Bay and the steel companies' wharves. Beside us was a rusty swing bridge which carried train traffic over the canal. I remembered visiting here as a kid and watching a gang of young daredevils jumping from the train bridge into the churning water after a big freighter passed through. But not me, Boy!

Across the bridge a line of smaller summer places dotted the lakeside on the Burlington side of the canal. Past these cottages you could see the Brant Inn with its outdoor dance floor, the Sky Club, built out over the water. I told Dave to make a left turn onto North Shore Boulevard where the QEW widened again to four lanes.

"What was that house number again, Max?"

"Number 492. But don't stop yet, we've still got 20 minutes before my appointment."

Dave drove slowly along this stretch of manicured lawns and sprawling bungalows with a spectacular view along the north shore of the bay. The homes became larger and were set further back from the roadway as we went further west. Many of the maples and birches here had lost their leaves, which allowed us to see across to the Hamilton side where the Stelco and Dofasco smokestacks exacted their price for good-paying jobs from the city's northern end.

"Goddamn," Dave said. "These are some swell houses. Great big buggers, ain't they?"

I asked him to slow down as we passed 492, a low fieldstone bungalow that must have had a dozen rooms and a three-car garage connected to the house by a covered walkway. A couple of gardeners were turning the soil in the flower beds bordering the driveway. I caught a glimpse of a boathouse and dock at the shoreline, a sleek wooden runabout still in the water. Sure as hell, Thomas Sherman wasn't standing in any pogey line.

Just past Sherman's home was the Burlington Golf and Country Club where, no doubt, he was a member. Despite the nippy breeze off the bay, several groups of older men were playing golf. A gilded sign beside the entrance proudly boasted: *Established 1922.*

Dave bobbed his head toward the golfers. "You ever try that game, Sarge?"

"Too rich for me. You join a club like that you've gotta have the right colour of blood."

About a mile further we entered LaSalle Park, turned around in the parking area and headed back to Thomas Sherman's home. Dave pulled into the circular drive and dropped me at the front door.

"Give me about an hour. You won't have any trouble keeping yourself amused, eh?"

He gave me a wolfish grin. "No trouble at all, Sarge. I got my eye on a certain waitress who works at a joint on Plains Road."

The gardeners stopped their digging to watch me get out of the cab and limp to the front door. So I waved in their direction and they went back to work. A fashionably dressed young woman answered the door with a smile. "Ah, you must be Mr. Dexter. And right on time. Here, let me take your hat."

I passed her my fedora. "Don't forget to give it back. It's a family heirloom."

She laughed out loud at my little joke as she placed the hat on a hall table. I didn't think it was that funny but I grinned at her.

"Mr. Sherman's in the den." She had a kind of singsong voice, one of those people who was perky from birth. "Walk this way," she said and swivelled her behind down a long hallway. I couldn't walk that way in a million years but I kept my lip buttoned and enjoyed the show as we approached the door at the end of the hall.

"You're Miss Scott, right?"

"Yes, I am, but no relation to Barbara Ann."

I guessed it was my turn to laugh so I gave her a hearty chuckle. "Thanks for your help. Maybe I'll see you later."

I entered Sherman's office and she closed the door behind me.

Sherman's den was a vast room, furnished with red leather armchairs and plush sofas arranged to take advantage of the bay view through the floor-to-ceiling windows. I now saw that the boathouse I'd glimpsed when we drove past was a substantial building: there was an apartment on its second level and on the lawn by the dock were several red canoes.

When we shook hands he gave me a bone-crusher, maybe to mark his territory, and he pointed to the big chairs by the windows.

"Looks like a summer resort," I said as I settled back and gawked at the view.

"Yes, it's a lovely spot." He'd crossed to the bar and set out a couple of glasses. The last time I'd seen him he was dressed in black for his father's funeral. Now he was decked out like the commodore of the Royal Hamilton Yacht Club – a sporty blue blazer and grey trousers. The red silk handkerchief sprouting from the jacket's pocket matched his flashy foulard. "What's your pleasure?"

"Just a cold beer, if you've got one."

He returned the glasses to their shelf and poured a couple of Peller's Ale into tankards. He passed me one as he sat in the chair beside me. "To your good health," he said and lifted his tankard to his lips. I wondered if he was trying to show me he was just one of the boys, drinking a good old Peller's after a hard day's work. I looked around at the splendour of his home. If this guy had done one day of hard work I'd eat my shorts.

"Good of you to see me, Mr. Sherman. And I offer my condolences again on the loss of your father."

"Thank you. But just call me Tom; after all, we're about the same age." He leaned back in his chair, crossed his legs and gave me an appraising look. His right leg was swinging slowly, the tassel on his shiny black loafer dancing up and down. "Now, what can I do for you?"

I took a long gulp of my Peller's and set it on the side table between us. "When we met after the funeral service I mentioned that a friend of mine was arrested for your father's murder. I'm convinced he didn't do it. So I'm trying to find some evidence to prove his innocence."

He sipped his beer but didn't seem to enjoy it. "The police told me your friend argued with my father about a painting, then they apparently struggled and he killed him. That sounds pretty straightforward to me, Dexter."

"It seems so, on the surface. But I'm sure you're as anxious as I am that the real killer is convicted."

His face remained expressionless, waiting for me to say my piece. I didn't have a firm objective in mind for this interview but I figured my new pal Tom was now in charge of the Sherman family fortune, so I was following Charlie Chan's advice to Number One Son: "Follow the money." And it was always surprising to me what people would tell you if they were asked nicely.

I sent him my Sunday smile. "So, I was wondering if you could tell me a little about your father's business interests. Perhaps there's a connection there."

He stared at me blank-faced, giving nothing away. "No connection I can think of. My grandfather and great-uncle were in the power transmission business for many years and their company passed to my father, who eventually sold it. Since then he was involved in real estate and land development and I joined him after graduating from Harvard."

Harvard, he said, as though it were a holy shrine and not a highfalutin diploma factory where rich kids spent a few years being polished up for a life of cognac, cigars and corporate flim-flammery. But maybe I was just jealous.

I gave him my sincere look, the one I use to pry information from reluctant interviewees. "These real estate and land deals. Can you tell me a little bit about how that works?"

He nodded right away, maybe pleased to show off his knowledge about the subject. "Well, sure. To put it in simple terms, we analyze business trends, looking for opportunities to expand into developing markets. Then we assemble tracts of land for certain interested parties. Housing and apartment complexes between here and Toronto will be a particularly lucrative investment in the near future." He leaned toward me and lowered his voice. "I'd advise investing in that market, Dexter, the sooner the better."

I grinned at him as though I were grateful for his insider's tip. But at least he was talking, so maybe I could steer him in my direction. "Sounds interesting. But I suppose there's a fair bit of competition in that business. And it must be risky forecasting these trends."

Thomas became more animated now. "That's the exciting part of the business. Being the first one to get to market with a better product. And you've got to be willing to take a chance on some of these deals. One wrong move and you might be stuck with a huge chunk of property whose value plummets. It's the challenge of the game, you see."

I noticed his cheeks were now glowing with excitement while he explained the real estate game to such a willing listener. The man loved an audience. "I suppose when you're putting together a really big project you might have to collaborate with other business partners."

He paused for a moment, maybe wondering if I knew something more than I was letting on. But I didn't think he could stop himself: he was on a roll now. "Well, sure, we do that from time to time. Sometimes you need a large infusion of cash to seal a deal – on a short-term basis, of course."

I looked at him with approval. He hadn't blurted out that he'd recently been short of cash and turned to Tedesco and company for an 'infusion', but I didn't expect him to. I decided to wrap up this interview and keep the door open for another time, if necessary. "It sure sounds like an exciting business, Tom. Was your father just as eager as you are?"

"Well, maybe in his prime. But in the last few years –" he paused, shaking his head. "He was beginning to show his age and he wasn't keeping up with trends in the market. I'm afraid he didn't recognize the time was ripe to work with new partners, to take the business in a new direction. Then last year he had a heart attack and was forced to retire."

I remembered Grace Clarke saying she'd told her son that Mr. Sherman had a heart attack to explain his death – to spare Vincent the shock of the grisly murder. But I hadn't realized Sherman actually had a previous heart condition.

"So he was probably pleased that you were there to take over. It must have allowed him to regain his health and to spend time with his art collection, knowing the business was in your capable hands."

He lapped up my compliment, giving me a broad smile and reaching over to pat me on the arm. "That's exactly right, Dexter. You know how the world works." Then he got to his feet, strode over to the bar and held up a bottle of *Crown Royal*. "I'm ready for a real drink. How about you?"

I held up my beer. "No thanks. I'll stick with this."

He poured a healthy shot into a highball glass and resumed his seat. He sampled his whisky then changed the subject. "I couldn't help noticing you walk with a limp. Were you injured during the war, if you don't mind my asking?"

"Don't mind at all. Yes, I took some shrapnel in my leg during the Normandy invasion – it's one of Jerry's little reminders. But it doesn't prevent me from doing most things." Then I thought about my performance on the dance floor at the Circus Roof. Well, I did say *most* things.

"How about you, Tom? Did you serve overseas?"

"I tried to enlist but I had rheumatic fever as a kid which left me with a damaged heart valve. It doesn't bother me too much so you can imagine my disappointment when I was rejected on medical grounds. Especially since my brother lost his life at Dieppe."

I gave him a sympathetic look but wondered if his father had pulled a few strings to keep him out of harm's way. Maybe deciding that the sacrifice of one son was enough of a contribution to the war effort. I'd heard that type of thing went on among Hamilton's high and mighty.

I finished my beer and placed my hands on the arms of the plush leather chair, pushing myself up. "Thanks for giving me so much of your time. I appreciate your hospitality."

He waved a hand to dismiss the idea. "Think nothing of it. Sorry I couldn't be more helpful."

I limped toward the door still wondering if Thomas was the man whom Vincent had seen from the bushes. He seemed to fill the bill – or it was someone very like him. As we were shaking hands at the doorway, I asked him, "I don't suppose I could see you again some time? For advice about investing in the real estate market?"

He laughed out loud and clapped me on the back. "Sure thing. Just call Marge and arrange it."

His secretary must have heard us speaking because she appeared from a room down the hallway.

"Marge will show you out," Thomas said and he closed the door to his den.

I stood with Marge on the front porch; we were pals now after chatting for a few minutes while waiting for my cab to return.

"You work for Mr. Sherman for long?"

She shook her head and her blonde curls danced like golden springs. "Almost a year."

I glanced at her face and noticed a few tiny wrinkles around her eyes and mouth; Marge wasn't right out of business college. "And during the war?"

"Oh, I had a great job, Max. I just loved it. At the Otis Elevator plant, you know, on Victoria Avenue. Instead of elevators, we were making those big Bofors anti-aircraft guns. I worked on the assembly with a bunch of other girls. Anyway, when the war was over and the men came home, the company went back to making elevators and the women were replaced by the veterans."

"Do you miss it, Marge?"

"You bet I do. But the men were risking their lives for us, so I guess it's only right that they should've gotten our jobs."

When Dave finally appeared I saw him ducking his head, looking for me. When he spotted Marjorie Scott, he was out of the car in a flash and hustled over to us.

"Hi there, Max. I'm right on time, as usual." He turned to Marge, showing her a broad smile and handed her a Veterans Cab business card. "Anytime you need a taxi, Miss, just give us a call and ask for Dave."

At the end of Sherman's driveway I told Dave to take a left.

"We goin' back to LaSalle Park, Sarge?"

"No, to the golf club next door."

He gave me a quizzical look and shrugged. "Okay, you're the boss."

We drove through the entranceway to the club's grounds and I pointed Dave toward the far corner of the parking lot, closest to Sherman's property.

"Park at the end of this row. We don't want to attract too much attention."

Dave stopped where I told him then riffled through a wad of papers attached to the cab's sun visor with two fat elastic bands. He withdrew an orange card, got out of the cab and snapped the card under the windshield wiper. I got out and walked around to his side to look at the card, which read: ON CALL.

"That keeps you from getting parking tickets? It's not even official."

"I know. But it works like a charm. Fancy joint like this, lotsa cars in the lot, it looks like I couldn't park any closer to the entrance so I left the cab down here and ran inside to look for my fare."

"You've got it all figured out, eh?" I slapped him on the back. "C'mon, let's go."

I led the way along the bay side of the road and through the bushes toward Sherman's home. I was panting when I limped to a stop behind a gnarled old maple and signalled Dave to come up beside me. From here we had a good view of the front of the house. "A special visitor's supposed to arrive soon," I said in a whisper. "I'd like to see who it is."

Dave grinned at me and kept his voice low. "So this is how a private dick works? Sneakin' around and spyin' on people?"

I gave him one of my hard stares but he continued to smile.

He said, "I think I might like this business."

We waited 10 minutes. Didn't have a good view back to the parking lot but I presumed nobody was bothered about the cab parked there. I checked my watch and precisely at 1700 a black Lincoln Continental rolled up Sherman's driveway and stopped at the front door. I squeezed Dave's arm, a finger to my lips for silence.

The driver opened his door and stepped out. A tall guy in his thirties, dressed in a smart black suit, his dark hair slicked back. He looked like a middleweight boxer. He opened a rear door and held it like a doorman.

Dominic Tedesco stepped from the car and took a moment to glance around at the house and the view across Burlington Bay. I'd only seen him from a distance and now, standing this close to him, I felt an electric jolt zip up my spine.

He was a tall man, dark-complexioned, and sturdily built, thick through the chest and arms. And a full head of black, wavy hair. As a young guy, Tedesco had worked for Rocco Perri and he was rumoured to be in on Rocco's mysterious disappearance, some say at the bottom of Burlington Bay. Since then, the bodies had been piling up in the wake of Tedesco's relentless rise to become the kingpin of the Hamilton Mob. I inhaled a deep breath, letting it out slowly, grateful that this powerful man didn't know I was sniffing around the edges of his criminal empire. Then I remembered Tom Sherman's boastful words and wondered if I was looking at the man who'd take the Sherman family business in a "new direction".

Dave tugged at my sleeve and whispered. "Holy shit! Is that who I think it is?"

I held up my hand for him to shut up and wait.

Marge opened the entrance door of the house and ushered the visitor inside. The driver walked around the car and rested his rump on the front fender while he fired up a cigarette and admired the million-dollar view. Looking at him in profile, I saw a certain resemblance to Thomas Sherman. And I wondered about the man Vincent saw from the bushes.

I tapped Dave on the arm, pointed with my finger toward the parking lot and made a zipping motion across my lips.

Back in the cab, Dave was puffing like he'd just received a sixty-yard pass from Frank Filchock and run it in for a touchdown. He kept looking behind us as he drove quickly from the golf club. "On second thought, I might not be cut out for this business."

CHAPTER TWENTY

When I returned to my office Phyllis was shrugging into a light raincoat, readying to leave for the day.

"Oh Max, I'm glad to see you. Isabel and *Robert* are still out interviewing witnesses for that Nelligan job. She said there was a problem and if they finish late they won't bother coming back to the office."

"Okay." I felt that tickle again at the back of my brain – what kind of problem? Why would they finish late? How late? Then my brain said – *Stop. You're jealous. It's a normal reaction. And you know what to do about it.*

Phyllis was holding my arm. "Are you all right, Max?"

"Sorry, I was just … thinking."

"Well, Sergeant Russo called. He said it wasn't urgent." Then she placed her purse over her arm and headed for the door. "Ta-ta for now, Max."

I smiled as I watched her leave. She was straight out of business school last summer but was learning fast under Isabel's guidance. And sounding more like her every day.

I flopped in my office chair and called Frank. He was in a chipper mood.

"How's tricks, Max? You haven't been buggin' me for a few days. You feelin' all right?"

"Funny, Frank. You called me."

"Yeah. I've gotta drop something off at the courthouse then I'm done for the day. Maybe we could meet at the Wentworth Arms for a beer. Twenty minutes?"

I snapped off the lights, put on my hat and headed for the elevator. As I was about to board it, Scotty Lyle stepped out and grabbed me by the arm.

"Just the man I want to see." His face was red and puffy and I could see he was working himself into a rant.

"Hang on, Unc. I'm on my way to an important meeting – it could be life or death. I promise I'll see you tomorrow for a full briefing."

He leaned against the wall, waving his cane at me like a swagger stick. "We had a deal, Laddie. And you're not keepin' your end of the bargain."

"Tomorrow." I backed away from him toward the elevator. "First thing in the morning."

Tiny, the operator, had kept the elevator door open and slammed it shut when I entered. "That man's going to bust a gasket," he said under his breath.

It was windy and cool on King Street where the after-work crowd was hustling to get home or into the bars and restaurants along this stretch. At the corner of Hughson I joined an anxious group of pedestrians waiting for a break in the traffic to cross the street.

An old-timer beside me said, "You'd think the damn City would've installed traffic lights at this intersection by now. You might get killed, for Pete's sake."

A Belt Line streetcar stopped to discharge passengers and I grabbed the old gent's arm. "Hang on tight. We'll risk it together."

Safely across, I limped up Hughson to Main Street and glanced across at the old stone courthouse. Then I entered the Wentworth Arms Hotel on the corner.

Through the haze of cigarette smoke I spotted Frank at a table near a window and he waved me over. When I sat he slid a full glass of beer toward me.

"My treat, Max. I'm in a good mood today."

"That's a change. How come?"

He dipped a finger into his glass and flicked a spray of suds my way. "Show a bit of gratitude, would ya? Angela was at the doctor's today. She's pregnant and the doc thinks it might be a girl."

I watched the grin spread across his big mug as though he'd performed some kind of miracle. But maybe I was just jealous. Jeez, that was twice in the past hour.

"I'm very happy for you, Frank. Is Angie doing well? I remember she had some trouble with the twins."

"She's fine. Doc says it'll be a lot easier this time."

I watched him swig his beer then swipe the back of his hand across his mouth, wiping away some foam. I was pleased for him; he was a devoted father and I reached across the table to shake his hand. "Congratulations, Frank. I mean it."

"About time you started thinkin' about a family, Max. You ain't gettin' any younger."

I gave him my blank stare, as though I had no idea what he was talking about.

"God, Max. Sometimes you're really dumb." He took another gulp of beer, set down his glass and sat straighter in his chair, which made me sense a change of subject. "Your pal Roger Bruce."

I raised my eyebrows. "Developments?"

"Not a helluva lot, I'm afraid. We had a screw-up at the office." He leaned toward me and lowered his voice; we were almost head to head. "If you breathe a word of this to anyone, you're dead."

"Scout's honour."

"I had to appear in court in Toronto last week; so I was gone all day Thursday and Friday. While I was on the stand testifying, the guy I'd lined up to keep the ball rolling in my absence went out on sick leave. So the captain assigned another guy, Bob Nichols ... you ever meet him?"

I shook my head.

"Well, he's a nice enough guy, but a lazy bugger; I'm trying to get him transferred to the Motorcycle Unit. So far, he'd phoned Sherman's son but didn't arrange to meet him yet. Then he spoke to the housekeeper at the Sherman home, Grace Clarke, and his report was identical to that of the first officers on the

scene. Finally, he went to visit the suspect in jail, found out he
was busy with his lawyer and never returned."

"Shit," I said.

"Shit is right. I saw your friend Roger today. He hasn't
wavered from his original statement, so at least he's consistent.
And he's got this bombshell babe of a lawyer now – Boy, what a
looker. She arrived when I was about to leave and those guys at
the jail had their tongues hangin' out. You know her?"

"You're a married man, your wife's pregnant. Again."

"No harm in lookin', eh?"

"Her name's Emma Rose. She's a head taller'n you, Bud, so
forget about her."

He was shaking his head, a dopey grin on his face.

"Have you met the son yet? Thomas Sherman?"

Frank got back to business. "He's been actin' scarce but I'll
get a hold of him tomorrow. And there's a lawyer who's lookin'
after the old man's estate. Guy by the name of Philip Neatby, got
an office up there in the Pigott Building. I'd like to see the will,
find out who gets what."

I'd like to see it too so I made a mental note of the lawyer's
name. "When'll you find out about the will?"

"This guy Neatby says there was a foul-up with probate or
some other legal foofaraw because Mr. Sherman had recently
revised his will. He says it'll be available tomorrow."

He recently revised his will. Why the hell would he do that, I
wondered. That image of Charlie Chan popped back into my
mind – and if I wanted to take his advice to 'follow the money' I
might have to take a detour.

I took a moment to gather my thoughts, thinking of how to
explain to Frank what Isabel and I had learned without getting
his nose out of joint – or mine, for that matter. "You know I've
been busy on this case, Frank. I'm glad it was assigned to you and
I'll tell you what we've learned so far."

Those dark Calabrian eyes held me in their grip and I hurried
on to avoid hearing about 'civilians' poking into police business.

"That painting which Roger examined for Sherman? We
spoke with the dealer in Toronto who sold it to him. It's probably
just a copy of the original and we don't think it has anything to

do with the murder. I'll give you the dealer's business card if you want to follow up."

No reaction from Frank.

"We also saw Grace Clarke and she repeated the same account which she'd given to the police who investigated the scene."

I didn't mention the ladies' wristwatch at James Jewellers because Frank had already dismissed its significance when he told me about it last week. So I kept quiet about our suspicion that it probably belonged to Grace.

"Grace has a nine-year-old son; his name's Vincent. And he's a pretty smart kid. I had a chance to speak with him alone and he told me he was playing outside with a friend about the time of the murder. He saw Roger Bruce leave the house, Frank."

I paused and took a long swig of beer while Frank held his tongue, quietly tapping his fingers on the table, so I continued. "Shortly after Roger left, the kid saw another man enter the house, stay a few minutes, then leave. He thought it looked like Thomas Sherman."

Now I watched Frank's jaw muscles tighten, probably biting back some choice words he couldn't use in a public place. He took a deep breath and his face relaxed, but not his mood. "When did you plan to report this to the police? After you wrapped up the case and got your picture in the *Spectator*?"

"I'm telling you now. You just got back on the case, for cryin' out loud. Now, do you want to hear the rest or not?"

Frank was a straight-ahead guy. I'd known him from childhood on Napier Street. So I knew that he never beat around the bush; he didn't know the meaning of subtlety or guile.

And now he spoke in a barely-controlled growl. "Just tell me what you know, for Chrissake. And whaddya mean the kid 'thought' the guy looked like Thomas Sherman? If it wasn't him, who the hell was it?"

"I don't know. And when I told Grace what her son saw, she was adamant that she wouldn't allow him to talk to the police. Too stressful for a young boy, she said." I leaned back in my chair and watched Frank's face pucker as though I'd spiked his beer with a dill pickle.

I waited a moment before saying, "And I didn't feel the timing was right to ask Thomas when I met him this afternoon."

I picked up my glass quickly and watched Frank's face over the rim as I drank. I was betting a lot on my belief that he wouldn't hit a guy while he was drinking his beer. But when I saw his cheeks bloom with frustration as he pushed his chair back and lean across the table, I figured I made a bum bet.

He growled at me. "Outside, Buster, we need to talk in private – where nobody can see me when I beat you to a pulp."

We crossed Hughson Street and sat on a park bench under a street lamp in front of the courthouse. The wind had died down and I felt a cold dampness in the air as we sat facing the flow of traffic.

"People can see us here, Frank. So forget about that beating."

He turned toward me and gave me a pitying look. "I don't know what you were thinking, Max. You know damn well you can't just muck around with witnesses in an ongoing case. Damnit all, you were a cop so you know the score. What would *you* say to a guy who pushed his way into your case because he thought he could do a better job than you? And don't tell me you wouldn't be pissed. You'd probably arrest the guy, charge him with interference, or worse."

I knew he had a point but I couldn't admit it. So I tried a bit of backpedalling. "You told me yourself the investigation was going nowhere with your stand-in. So I had to do something. And things just ... happened."

I hadn't seen him quite this angry since that time when I was in his family's place on Napier Street and I walked into his bedroom without knocking, his high school sweetheart bare-ass on the bed with him and his mother gaping beside me.

"We've gotta work together, Frank. Now that you're on this case, I'll keep you up to date on our work. And I hope you'll do the same."

His expression changed from front-burner anger to a medium simmer. "You know I can't tell you everything, Max. It's just the way it is." He shifted a bit closer to me. "Now show me a sign of your co-operation. Tell me if there's anything else you've been up to."

I looked him in the eye: Frank Russo was an honest man, a family man. And my best friend. And we had a deal. "There's one other thing, Frank."

His eyes began to spin and he nudged away from me, fidgety and about to get wound up again. "Relax," I said, grabbing his arm. "I'm levelling with you. Doing what you asked me to do."

"Okay, what is it?"

"I was out at Thomas Sherman's house in Burlington; he lives on the north shore, beside that fancy golf course. According to his secretary he's working from his home now, not using his office downtown. So I get out there and he gives me a drink and we have a little chinwag and he proceeds to tell me about the land development business and what a growing market it is and it's a perfect time for me to invest in it. I didn't want to lean on him, Frank. I was just looking to build a little trust between us so he might open up a bit more. But he didn't and I decided to leave it for another time."

Frank was nodding as I spoke, listening intently. Then I noticed his face tightening as though he was readying himself for a punchline he wouldn't like. "And ..."

"And after I left, I circled the property and found a hidden spot where I could watch his front door and observe his next visitor."

"And ..." Frank said it louder this time.

"It was Dominic Tedesco."

He didn't explode as I thought he would. He didn't say a damn word for a full minute, just glared at me, shaking his head from side to side. I waited.

Finally, he let out an exasperated croak, "Well, if that doesn't take the fur-lined piss-pot."

I had to force myself, but I remained silent, waiting for his frustration to run its course.

Then he rose from the bench and pulled me to my feet. "Maybe it's true what they say, Maxie. Maybe you're one of those guys who's an accident waiting to happen."

CHAPTER TWENTY-ONE

WHEN I LOOKED OUT MY kitchen window the following morning, a brisk wind had swept a pile of dried leaves against the door, almost covering a quart of Royal Oak milk. Since the milkman was always late I knew I'd slept in again, damnit. I blamed it on the change of seasons. I retrieved the milk from the stoop and put it in the icebox. Yesterday's *Spec* said the cost of milk was going to rise from 16 to 18 cents a quart. And that same article suggested the ten-cent chocolate bar was not far off. What the hell next, I wondered.

I'd arranged to see Roger Bruce at the jail first thing this morning, so I made short work of my Grape Nuts, slurped down a cup of Maxwell House and was outside my ground-floor apartment on Emerald Street when the Veterans Cab I called rolled to the curb.

At the Barton Street Jail, the same old bird was manning the front desk. He took his sweet time filing a piece of paper in a cabinet beside his desk, then lowered the volume of his mantle radio. But not low enough; I could still hear the syrupy voice of Perry Como crooning *Prisoner of Love*.

I said, "Must be a big favourite here, eh?"

"Huh?"

"The song. On the radio."

He was staring at me, mystified. "Forget it," I said. "I arranged to see a prisoner this morning, Roger Bruce, and I'm a bit late. Can I see him now?"

"'Fraid not."

"What the hell?"

"Profanity isn't called for."

I now noticed a small crucifix on the wall by his desk and figured that, in addition to being a stickler for the jail's rules, he was probably the same in his religious beliefs.

"Excuse me. But why can't I see Roger Bruce?"

"He's busy with his lawyer."

"Oh. Any idea when they'll be finished?"

"'Fraid not."

"Well, thank you very much for your help. Do you mind if I just wait here until he's free?"

He gave me a blank look. "Suit yourself."

While I was cooling my heels on a hard wooden chair, I noticed a quick young guy, maybe in his mid-twenties, dressed in a smart blue suit, bustling in and out through a door marked "Administration". I stood up and stopped him on his next pass through the waiting area.

"Pardon me," I said, waving him over. "You got a minute?"

"Sure. What can I do for you?"

"You work here, right? In administration?"

He gave me a wary look. "Yeah. Why?"

I pointed to the row of chairs. "Mind if we sit?"

We sat beside each other and I extended my hand. "Max Dexter. I'm a private investigator and one of my clients is in custody here."

We shook hands. "Eddie Ryan. Pleased to meet you."

I looked at him more closely now and saw a kind of darkness in his eyes; like the guys I'd seen returning from the battlefront. Here was a man who had seen death and suffering. A lengthy scar wormed along the left side of his neck. "You been here long, Eddie?"

"After I was discharged, I was lucky enough to get this job, almost two years now. They sent me for some courses in Toronto and I worked a few months at the Don Jail. It's interesting work."

It wouldn't have been my cup of tea, but to each his own. "Where'd you serve?"

"I was with the Hastings and Prince Edward Regiment –"

"The Hasty P's."

"That's right. I joined up in '39 and after training we were in Sicily for a couple of years, then joined up with Monty's 8th Army in Italy. Then we were deployed to Western Europe until the end of the war."

Something was niggling at the back of my mind while he spoke and it came to me. "You were the guys who were called the 'D-Day Dodgers'."

"Yeah, we were. Because we weren't in Normandy on D-Day we were called dodgers – supposedly having an easy time of it down there in Italy while the real fighting was up north."

"You got a bum rap, Eddie."

"We sure did. But one of the guys composed a sarcastic reply in a song to the tune of *Lili Marlene*. We still sing it when we get together."

I gestured with my chin toward the scar on his neck. "Looks like you finished the war with a little reminder."

"Landing in Sicily. Woke up on a British hospital ship, all bandaged up, and this young nurse says, 'You'll be right as rain, Dearie. How about a nice cuppa?'"

We both laughed and he pointed to my leg. "Saw you limping when you arrived."

"Provost Corps. Dieppe then Normandy – that's where I caught a chunk of Jerry's shrapnel. While you were sunning yourself in Italy."

He laughed at my jibe and gave me a soft jab on the shoulder. "So what're you sittin' out here for?"

"Like I said, I'm here to see my client; he's being held for suspicion."

"Suspicion of what?"

"Murder. But he didn't do it. And I'm gathering information to get him released."

"Ah, so your client's Roger Bruce."

"Yeah. How'd you know?"

"We don't get many prisoners charged with murder. We're a small operation here. People sentenced to two years or more are shipped off to the Kingston Pen. So our inmates are serving time for lesser crimes; burglary, drunk and disorderly, shoplifting, that type of thing. Winter's our busy season – when the old guys from Gore Park commit their petty crimes so they can come in from the cold for a month or two. We call those guys 'the old faithfuls' around here. But getting back to your client, we'll only keep him here as long as his trial lasts and if he's convicted we'll move him on. Just like Evelyn Dick."

I stood up and he followed suit. "Well, my client's meeting with his lawyer," I said. "And I'm waiting for him."

His eyes opened wide. "I saw his lawyer. In fact, **Everybody** saw his lawyer. She's a real humdinger, isn't she?"

I grinned at him and, as if on cue, Emma Rose emerged from a hallway to our left.

Emma approached and stood beside Eddie, towering over him. We exchanged hellos and I asked Eddie, "Would it be all right if I spoke with Miss Rose and Roger Bruce in the lawyer's room for a few minutes?"

Eddie glanced over at the guard at his desk, who was pretending not to listen, his radio off, and a scowl on his puss. Then Eddie turned back to me. "No can do, Bud. Rules are made for a reason, no exceptions."

Emma was watching our exchange and sensed my frustration. "Mr. Dexter's part of our defence team and I can vouch for him."

"Sorry, Miss. Nothing against your investigator, but we have a system and we stick by it. Now I'll wish you both good day." He gave us a brief bow and hustled off through the Administration door.

The old boy at his desk didn't try very hard to hide his smirk. He said, "Just take a seat there and I'll notify you when the prisoner has been taken to his cell."

I wanted to cross the room and give him a swift kick but held myself in check. I turned to Emma. "Let's have a chat outside."

We stood in an alcove beside the entrance to protect us from the cool wind. "These buggers are fanatical about their damn regulations. Worse than the Vatican."

She laughed at my annoyance. "This is no place for you, Max. A guy with a reputation for making a pretzel of the rules."

"Well, it's maddening. I wanted to tell you and Roger about a witness we've found. So if you've got some time, maybe I could speak with you now and I'll see Roger later."

"Who's the witness, Max?"

"He's the nine-year-old son of Grace Clarke, the housekeeper at the Sherman place. On the afternoon of the murder he was playing with a friend down the street and he says he saw Roger leaving the house. Then shortly afterward another man entered the house, stayed a few minutes and left. The boy thought it looked like Thomas Sherman but he wasn't certain."

Her coat collar was turned up and she clutched it tightly with her fist as a gust of wind swirled past us. "Well, that's good news. If he's a credible witness that could be the break we need."

I shook my head. "His mother doesn't want him to speak to the police. Says it would be too upsetting, but I think there might be something else going on. I was wondering if minors could be compelled to come forward."

"There's no law saying the police can't talk to him. To my knowledge, Hamilton police officers will usually contact a minor's parent if the minor is to be charged with an offence. But if the minor's only a witness, they often don't. So in this case, an officer would likely go to see the housekeeper, explain the situation to her and interview the boy."

"What about testifying in court? Could her son be subpoenaed to testify if his mother objects?"

"Yes. But that doesn't happen often."

I thought about her answer for a moment. "We'll have to explain this police policy to Grace very carefully. And once she understands it I hope she'll be co-operative."

"You should report this to the police, Max. Roger said you were a friend of Sergeant Russo and it's his case, so ..." She bent her head a little, looking me in the eye. "You can't do this all on your own, Sherlock; your pal in there is depending on you. And I can't go to the Crown Attorney and argue for bail without some evidence."

I raised my eyes to hers, showing her my long-suffering, patient look I reserve for dimwits. And I waited.

She squinted at me. "What's going on, Max?"

"I spoke with Frank Russo yesterday, thank you, and I told him all this. Also, for your information, he told me he spoke with Sherman's lawyer about his will. He'd recently revised it and Frank should have a copy soon – maybe later today."

Emma's face crinkled into a wide smile and she gave me a solid whack in the arm. "Just like old times, isn't it, Max? I'd forgotten that you're a lot craftier than you look. And getting better at it, too." Her smile faded when she got back to business. "Who's the lawyer?"

"Name's Neatby. In the Pigott Building."

She bobbed her head. "I know him. His office is on the floor below mine. I might just pay him a visit when I get back. Anything else from Frank Russo?"

"Nope. And I'll expect your call as soon as you get word about the will."

When Emma left I re-entered the jail and approached my favourite guard. "Back again. Would you be kind enough to accompany me to Roger Bruce's cell, please?"

He didn't answer right away and I kept my trap shut.

"Sarcasm won't win you any friends here."

"Noted." I paused a beat. "Roger Bruce."

As he led the way to the holding cells, he spoke over his shoulder. "I met a few young guys like you when I served in the Great War. They knew it all – thought they were bulletproof; you couldn't tell them a thing. Some of them weren't even wearing their gas masks when we were hit with the mustard gas."

He turned to face me. "Just remember: there's a big difference between a wise man and a wise guy." Then he took up his post while I limped over to Roger's cell.

Roger glanced toward the guard. "Gettin' friendly with that guy, Max?"

I gave him a grin. "I'm friendly with everyone. Even you."

A chagrined look on his mug. "I'm still feeling like a horse's ass for not coming clean with you, Max. I promise it'll never happen again."

"I believe you. Now let's put that behind us." I glanced over at the guard. He seemed to be following our conversation so I turned sideways, my back toward him. "There's been a development. The housekeeper's son saw you hustling out of Sherman's house that day –"

"Yeah, so ...?"

"After you'd gone he saw another man enter, stay a couple of minutes then leave."

He pressed himself against the wire mesh between us, his eyes ablaze. "Now we're gettin' somewhere, Max. So the kid must have spotted the killer; who was it?"

"He says it looked like Thomas Sherman, the old man's son, but he couldn't be sure. Now I'm looking into Thomas's background and I've talked to him a couple of times. He's certainly a suspect in my book."

"Well, let's get the cops after him. He should be in here instead of me, goddamnit."

"We're on the job, Roger. It's not that simple, so try to be patient."

I saw him roll his eyes and he took a couple of deep breaths to steady himself. Watching his frustration made me kick myself in the pants for advising him to "be patient". If our situations were reversed would I have listened to the guy on the other side of the bars when he gave me that worthless advice?

Before he could speak again, I changed the subject. "Emma Rose is dogging the Crown Attorney to get you out on bail. We're lucky to have her working with us. You gettin' along with her all right?"

It surprised the hell out of me when I saw a goofy grin creep across his mug. I hadn't seen him smile, or anything close to it, since this nightmare began for him. "What's up, Bud? What'd I say?"

"Emma's the one bright spot in this whole damn thing." That stupid grin stayed in place as he continued. "She's quite a woman, Max. Brains and ... well, and everything else."

Holy Mackerel! I couldn't believe my ears. The guy's arrested for murder, locked in a stinking cell and he's suddenly going gaga over his lawyer. Maybe it's true that love knows no boundaries – but I thought it more likely that Roger's fascination with Emma was his way of dealing with his godawful situation.

"So, Romeo. You've got eyes for your mouthpiece?"

He didn't speak but his face said, 'Yeah, I sure as hell do.'

I buttoned my coat, getting ready to leave. "I want you to know we're doing everything we can to get you of here. Try to hold on as best you can."

"Thanks, Max. Thanks for everything."

I touched my forehead in a small salute. "Okay, Pal. Keep your pecker up."

CHAPTER TWENTY-TWO

WHEN I RETURNED TO MY office, Phyllis was alone, seated on the couch by the window, eating a sandwich and reading a magazine. She looked up and gulped, taking a moment to swallow. "Sorry, Max, I didn't know when to expect you. *Robert* is interviewing witnesses and Isabel's having lunch with a friend. She left a sandwich on your desk."

I waved away her apology and went through to my office. On my desk were two stacks of papers – one a pile of business letters, the other some kind of accounting statements. On a plate beside these was a corned beef sandwich and a dill pickle with a note attached. It read, "I've reserved the afternoon to review our financial situation. I'll be back by one o'clock. Don't go anywhere."

I slumped into my chair and unwrapped the sandwich, imagining Isabel wagging a warning finger at me as she wrote that note. Shit – I was in for an afternoon of fun with the books.

Next morning I made a detour on my way to the office. It was 08:30 when I limped into Scotty's cubicle at the *Spectator* where he was bent over his typewriter, two-fingering his way through a story on God-knows-what nefarious scheme he'd uncovered. A forgotten cigarette had burned to a tubular strip of ash in a saucer beside him.

"I'm suing for libel," I said in a loud voice.

His head snapped up and he spun his chair to face me. "God, you startled me, Laddie. And what are you after, so early in the day?"

"Not after anything, Unc. I'm here to brief you, just as we agreed."

His eyes searched for his cigarette, saw the ash in the saucer, and he fired up another Winchester from a pack in his shirt pocket. "This should be good. You're only six days overdue. You've given me bugger all so far."

"First of all, Roger Bruce is not happy in jail."

He humphed.

"Emma Rose has been in to see him several times. She's a real crackerjack and Roger's damn lucky you got her to take his case."

He made a come-along motion with his hand. "Details. Gimme details."

"We checked on that painting I told you about, the one which Roger examined for Mr. Sherman, and it doesn't appear to be connected to his murder. But there are other factors at play."

"What other factors?"

I felt that familiar jolt of anger whenever I tried to bargain with this gruff Scot. I stepped closer, placing my hands on the edge of his desk, and stretched my neck so we were face to face. "That's what we're working on now." Then I stood up and took a couple of deep breaths. "I've spoken with the dead man's son, Thomas. He took over the family business when his father developed a heart condition last year. And he's the executor of the estate. Had a long talk with the housekeeper and she was busy with some gardeners outside so she didn't see Roger Bruce or anyone else leaving the premises. And I didn't get anything from those gardeners either."

"That's it? Sounds to me like you haven't got a damn lead yet."

"Then you'd be wrong. We've got a couple of leads we're working. But we're not sure how they'll develop. These things take time, Unc. You know that."

He scowled as he stubbed out his cigarette in his makeshift ashtray. "Shit."

"I can't do all your work for you. Tell me what you've come up with."

He gave me the famous Scotty glower but I was developing immunity to it and I forced myself to smile, waiting him out.

"Had a beer with the Crown Attorney," he finally said. "He's charging your friend with second-degree and he's confident it'll stick. Talked to Emma a couple of times and she's nearly as good as you are at feeding me non-information. I'm still rooting around in the Sherman family closet but no skeletons yet. The old man was speculating in the land development game and there are rumours the Mob is washing its cash in that same market, so I thought I was onto something fishy ... but so far I haven't found any connection to Sherman."

I watched him sagging in his chair, frustration oozing out of his pores. But I was heartened to hear that Scotty also considered Sherman might've been involved with laundering Mob money. Of course, I wasn't going to tell him that.

I was on my feet now, backing away from him. "Okay, Unc. I've gotta run. Maybe we'll both have more to report tomorrow."

At my office I shucked off my raincoat and hung it on the rack by the door, cursing the CKOC weather guy for his forecast, which was no better than the one on CHML. Are these radio guys ever right?

I didn't see Trepanier so I figured he was out on the interviewing job. But I heard Isabel and Phyllis talking in my office. As I approached, Phyllis was saying, "... and *Robert's* so dreamy, isn't he?"

I stopped in my tracks, thinking: is there no limit to this guy's charm with the ladies? I didn't say that, of course, but entered the office. "Good morning," I said and turned to Iz. "I'm a bit late because I was giving Scotty a briefing." Then I made an exaggerated shudder.

"He's not that bad, Max. And he is your only uncle." Then she hefted a couple of the big accounting ledgers, passed them to Phyllis and pointed her head toward the doorway. "Just put them on the long table. I'll be with you in a minute."

I sat at my desk and Iz drew up the visitor's chair. "What's on the agenda today, Boss?"

I studied the wry smile on her face. She'd been calling me 'Boss' since we'd had our discussion about hiring Trepanier and

I felt I was missing something here. "Are you trying to tell me something with this 'Boss' business?"

She widened her eyes in mock surprise. "Now why would I do that?"

I stopped myself right there. I'd known her long enough to realize I wasn't holding a winning hand here. "Okay. Could you call Grace, please? See if we could see her this morning about going to the police about Vincent's information. Just say – well, you know what to say."

CHAPTER TWENTY-THREE

IT WAS A DIFFERENT GRACE Clarke who opened the front door at the big house on Park Street this morning. Her dark eyes had lost their sparkle and, as we followed her to the kitchen, she seemed listless – no spring in her step, no trace of the self-confident, energetic Grace we'd met before.

We sat at the big table again. But there was no coffee on offer, just as there was no welcome in Grace's icy manner.

"You were kind to me when we met before," she said. "It's the only reason I've agreed to see you now. Miss O'Brien explained your purpose on the phone. But I just can't subject my boy to police questioning or, God forbid, testifying in court. It's too much to ask of a mother."

I almost opened my mouth but Isabel touched my arm and I sat back.

"We know it's a difficult thing we're asking you to do, Grace. But you and your son have been given a rare opportunity here. Your information will result in the police widening their investigation. And when they find this new suspect we believe they'll have found the man who killed Mr. Sherman." Isabel now reached for Grace's hand and held it tightly. "You and Vincent may save an innocent young man from spending the best years of his life in prison."

After a brief silence she released Grace's hand and leaned back in her chair.

Grace fidgeted, obviously touched by Isabel's plea. She withdrew a handkerchief from her sleeve and held it tightly in her hand, then pushed back her chair and walked to the window, staring at the bleak garden.

Still looking through the window, her back to us, Grace asked, "Would we have to testify in court?"

From the corner of my eye I watched Isabel exhaling the breath she'd been holding and the tension lines in her face relaxing.

Grace returned to the table and I leaned toward her. "You may not have to appear in court. But that decision is down the road. It depends on this new suspect being found. But at the very least, Vincent's testimony will cast serious doubt on the Crown Attorney's case against Roger Bruce."

Grace was squinting, considering my answer. "But if we didn't speak to the police now, could we be subpoenaed to appear in court later?"

"Yes, I believe so. But I'm not a lawyer and that's something we'd have to find out."

Grace appeared to be examining her fingernails, absently picking at some loose nail polish or something but, no doubt, trying to decide what was best for herself and her son. Then she raised her head to meet my gaze. "Would we have to go to the police station?"

I shook my head, sensing that she was close to deciding to see the police. "The officer in charge is a good friend of mine. He'll come here to the house to speak with you both."

Grace continued to fidget. Several times she opened her mouth to speak, then closed it without saying a word.

"Look. It's not that simple," she said at last. "When I came to Toronto from Jamaica I had a six-month visa. And like many foreign visitors I just stayed on after my visa expired. Then I got married, gave birth to Vincent, then that horrible war and Owen was killed ... well, I just never got around to applying for citizenship. I wasn't even sure I'd be eligible. Husbandless Jamaican mothers who work as domestics don't have much standing in Canada."

Isabel said, "So you're here illegally."

"That's right. And if it's brought to the attention of the authorities I could be deported. And I'm afraid of what might happen to Vincent."

Isabel moved her chair closer to Grace and again took hold of her hand. "And that's why you didn't want to speak with the police or appear in court."

"Yes, and I know it's my own fault. I should have looked after this problem years ago. But now, with Mr. Sherman's death …"

Her remark puzzled me. "Was he involved with your citizenship, Grace?"

She took a moment before she answered, as though she were still weighing our trustworthiness. "Mr. Sherman had his lawyer arranging for my Landed Immigrant status. I don't know what will happen with that now."

"Did he mention the lawyer's name?"

"Yes. It was Mr. Neatby."

I looked at Isabel and tilted my head.

She caught my signal and said to Grace, "He's also looking after Mr. Sherman's will. And the lawyer representing Roger Bruce is acquainted with him. So we could ask her to check with him about your immigration application."

Grace exhaled. "Could you? I'd be so relieved to have that problem fixed. You have no idea how worrisome it's been for me. I don't want to leave and I want Vincent to grow up here."

"We'll look into it right away," I told her. "But it's important that you speak to the police now."

She straightened in her chair, a determined look on her face. "Yes, I'm ready."

When we returned to the office I called Frank at the cop shop. "Grace Clarke's agreed to talk with you."

"Well, well, if it ain't Max Dexter, the Hamilton Police Department's best friend. Getting an early start on doing my job for me today?"

I bit back a smartass remark. "You're welcome, Frank. Anything else you need just give me a call."

The line went silent for a moment. "How did you get her to change her mind?"

"Credit where it's due – it was actually Isabel who convinced her it was the right thing to do. And we told her you'd go to her home to speak with her and her son."

"Yeah, I can do that. And if you behave yourself I just might let you know how it goes."

CHAPTER TWENTY-FOUR

I SAT AT MY DESK, shuffling through some notes I'd made about the Sherman family and their shenanigans. Sherman Senior and Grace seemed to be linked by that wristwatch. But what really went on between them? Sherman Junior might be playing footsies with Tedesco on some kind of land deal. Then Sherman Senior is murdered and his will ... Damn. I'd forgotten to call Emma Rose this morning about that will.

She came on the line after the first ring and I explained what I was after.

"Yes, I had a little chat with Mr. Neatby. He told me about the will and something else as well."

"Something else?"

"That's right. I'm heading off to court now but why don't you and Isabel meet me at the Connaught for lunch and we can talk about it?"

We risked our lives again crossing King Street at the corner of John. That old guy was right – there really should be a traffic signal there, or at least a cop.

Isabel and I entered the dining room at the Royal Connaught and I spotted Emma Rose chatting with the maître d' near the bar. She waved at us and we were shown to a private table near the back of the elegant room.

When the waiter approached it didn't surprise me that it was Longo. I wasn't a frequent customer but every time I came here, there was Longo. He handed a menu to Emma with a bow and said, "Miss Rose. Nice to see you." And another to Isabel. "Miss O'Brien. Welcome back." As he passed one to me, he tilted his

head toward the two women then fluttered his eyebrows like
Groucho Marx at me. "And you, Sir. I see you're doing very well."

We ordered the seafood special with white wine and got
down to business.

I looked at Emma, a designer's model today in a blue silk fit-
ted suit. "So you had a chat with Mr. Neatby."

"I did indeed. We're old friends and he's happy to share information with me from time to time."

"The will," I said.

She wagged a long finger at me. "Patience, my boy. All in
good time." Then she took a dainty sip of wine, her pinky finger
in the air, and I thought, she could make a very nice living on the
stage. "Mr. Neatby invited me for a drink at Fischer's after work
yesterday. And surprised me with a copy of the will."

Isabel was enjoying Emma's performance, smiling and sipping her wine. "But isn't that unethical, Emma? Passing around
someone's will?"

"Oh, not between lawyers. Especially if they have an
understanding."

Isabel looked my way and rolled her eyes. I couldn't believe
it either. It didn't sound kosher to me but I wasn't going to
quibble. "Just give us the juicy bits. We don't need all the legal
gobbledygook."

Our food arrived and Longo left. He may have been a petty
crook but he was a damn good waiter.

Emma tasted her fish before continuing. "In a nutshell,
Grace Clarke gets all the money, stocks and bonds. The Anglican
Diocese of Niagara gets all the investment land. And Thomas
Sherman gets the house on Park Street. Oh, by the way – Thomas
is no longer the executor. In the new will, it's Mr. Neatby."

Isabel sat back, eyes wide and gasping, "I don't believe it."

I was stunned too. Holy Moley, what a kick in the pants for
Thomas. And what a bonanza for Grace.

Emma set her wineglass down and leaned forward. "Mr.
Neatby is meeting with Grace and Thomas at noon today." She
glanced at her watch. "Right now, in fact."

I ignored my seafood and took a gulp of wine. "Does Mr.
Neatby know why Sherman changed his will?"

Emma shook her head. "If he does, he didn't tell me."

Isabel had picked up her wineglass but set it back down. She turned to Emma. "Oh, my. What a shocker. I guess Thomas won't be too pleased."

"Don't feel too sorry for him," Emma said. "Mr. Neatby told me he has a very healthy trust fund left to him by his grandfather. But I'll bet he's more surprised than we are."

I thought about this strange turn of events. My mind went back to Thomas telling me about land development and I wondered if he'd already made plans for his father's land. Plans which would now fall through. And if those plans involved Dominic Tedesco, well, Thomas was at risk of taking a one-way trip to the bottom of Burlington Bay, where he'd join the ranks of all those other guys who couldn't deliver on their end of a deal with Tedesco.

Emma hadn't finished her report. "There's one other item from Mr. Neatby – Mr. Sherman had asked him months ago to look into Grace's immigration status."

Isabel leaned forward. "Yes, I was supposed to call you about that. What's the latest?"

"Good news. She's been granted Landed Immigrant status."

"That's wonderful. It's been such a worry for her. May we tell her about it?"

Emma nodded. "Sure. Mr. Neatby will send her the documents."

Longo cleared our plates away. "Dessert is crème brûlée today, unless you'd prefer something else with your coffee."

When we'd finished our lunch, Emma and Isabel went to the ladies' room – to "freshen up", they said.

Longo returned with the bill and I nearly fell over when I looked at it. "Holy shit, Man! Is that what they get for the grub here?"

He smiled, nodding his head. "Yeah, it's a crime, ain't it?"

I pulled out my wallet and emptied it to cover the bill.

"And the tip?"

"Next time, Bud. That's the last of my do-re-mi."

Longo chuckled as he scooped up the bills. "You asked me to keep an eye out for Thomas Sherman, remember, Sarge?"

"Yeah."

"Well, he was here last night. Made a horse's ass of himself in the bar. Got belligerent and it took two of us to wrestle him outta there."

I thought about Sherman's will and I guessed that Mr. Neatby had delivered the bad news to Thomas yesterday, ahead of his scheduled meeting with Grace and Thomas today. "What was the ruckus about? D'you know?"

"Nope. But I saw a couple beefy guys come in and talk to him for a few minutes, then they left. Sherman got pretty agitated after that."

I stood and clapped him on the back. "Thanks."

Isabel and Emma returned and we walked out together. I looked back over my shoulder and saw Longo give that chef's kissing motion with his fingertips to his lips as he ogled the women with me.

CHAPTER TWENTY-FIVE

BACK AT MY DESK, I phoned Marjorie Scott at Sherman's office in the Lister Block, thinking they might be back at work – no answer. When I called his home, Marge answered and we chatted about the weather for a moment before I got down to business. "I thought you'd moved back downtown. So I called your office."

"Well, things are still topsy-turvy here. Mr. Sherman says we'll be working out of the house for the next while. Gee, I thought he was handling his father's death pretty well, but now he seems so ... well, agitated, I guess you'd say."

"Because of his father."

"That's what I thought at first. But now ... well, I just don't know what's got him in such a tizzy."

"Did they get along well, Marge? Thomas and his father?"

"They used to. But these past few months, they seemed to be arguing all the time."

I guessed that might be the case, especially if Tedesco's reputation was known to Sherman Senior. "Is Thomas still attending his business meetings?"

"No, not very many. But that nice Mr. Tedesco was back to see him again. About the contracts for a land deal."

That nice Mr. Tedesco. If she only knew. "Is your boss there now, Marge?"

"No, he's meeting his lawyer again this afternoon."

Again? So he did meet with him yesterday.

"Mr. Neatby."

She giggled. "Say, you're pretty smart, Max. Yes, Mr. Neatby is the family lawyer and he wanted to see Thomas about his father's will."

I figured Thomas would now have Mr. Neatby working over-time to find a way to have that will overturned. "Oh, by the way, Marge. Do you happen to have your boss's calendar handy or is it still in the office downtown?"

"No, it's right here. Did you want me to check something for you?"

I couldn't believe how helpful she was. And I confess to a small guilt pang for taking advantage of her trusting nature. "Well, if it's no trouble."

"No trouble at all. What was the date?"

"A week ago last Monday."

"Okey-dokey, let me see here. Oh, that's when he was in Toronto. Yes, he met with some government people about a land holding he was interested in."

I was wondering if Thomas had an alibi for that afternoon when Vincent thought he might have seen him.

"You absolutely sure he was in Toronto, Marge?"

"Well, of course, I'm sure. I was with him because he wanted me to take notes at his meeting."

"All afternoon in Toronto."

"And the evening too. We went to the King Eddy for dinner afterward."

Shit. So Vincent must've seen someone who looked like Thomas entering the Sherman house after Roger Bruce left. I reluctantly scratched Thomas off my list of suspects.

"You've been a big help, Marge. Thanks a lot."

"Anytime," she said. "Toodle-oo."

I hung up the phone and leaned back in my chair, propping up my bum leg across the bottom drawer. Marge said Thomas seemed agitated. And Longo said he created a scene at the Connaught's bar last night. I couldn't help thinking that *nice Mr. Tedesco* was giving Thomas the heebie-jeebies.

Frank called later in the afternoon. I was hoping he'd give me a sitrep after he'd met with Grace Clarke and Vincent.

"How did it go with the reluctant witnesses, Frank?"

"Better than I thought. At first, it was like pulling teeth but Grace loosened up later. And Vincent's a good boy – he'd be very believable in court if it came to that."

"I'm glad to hear it. I was worried she'd get cold feet and clam up on you."

"You shouldn't have worried, Bud. She responded well to my natural charm."

"Okay, so you did a good job. Did you find out about Sherman's will yet?"

"I did. Mr. Neatby called me after he'd met with Thomas and Grace. And he sent a copy to my office."

"Well, what about it? C'mon, out with it." It wouldn't help me if Frank knew I'd already learned the contents of the will. If I'd spilled the beans he would've gone into his familiar rant against 'those damn lawyers' and I didn't need another dose of that today.

"A helluva surprise – Grace's head is still whirling because Sherman left her all his money and securities. He owned some large tracts of land which he left to the Anglican Church and Thomas got the Park Street house."

I did a pretty good job of faking my shock. "Holy Hell! Grace must have been speechless. And I'll bet Thomas shit a brick. What did she say about that?"

"You're right. She said she was still stunned when Thomas stormed out of the meeting and didn't come back. The lawyer went after him but he was gone."

"I've been getting a creepy feeling about this Thomas guy, Frank. Remember I told you about the spiel he gave me about land development and all that stuff? And then I saw Tedesco at his house? Well, now I hear from Thomas's secretary that he's already in bed with Tedesco to do a land deal. Probably so Tedesco could build apartments or whatever in order to launder his moolah."

Frank took a moment before answering. "You could be right, Maxie. And maybe now Thomas doesn't have the land he thought he did. What would you do if you were in Thomas's shoes?"

"Well, I wouldn't appeal to Tedesco's good nature. I'd prob- ably leave the country – maybe move to Newfoundland so I'd still have some contact with Canada."

"Yeah, you might last a little longer there. But sooner or later …"

"I know, Frank. I don't like Thomas's chances."

CHAPTER TWENTY-SIX

I SAT AT MY DESK still thinking about Thomas and Tedesco and their plans to do a deal for the Sherman land. Then it occurred to me that they might have had a history of working together. A written history.

I checked my watch – 16:30. I phoned the Land Registry Office in the Provincial Building and learned they closed at 17:00.

I limped to the Provincial offices with 20 minutes to spare and asked for someone in Land Registry. A white-haired gent emerged from a back office and approached the long counter where I stood. He wore a red-striped dress shirt with a putrid green tie patterned with lily pads, which I tried to ignore. Who buys a lily pad tie?

"Help you?" he spoke in a tone which meant that help was the last thing he wanted to give me.

I explained that I'd like to see the Land Registry files concerning transactions along the Queen Elizabeth Way between Burlington and Oakville during the last year. And I slid one of my business cards across the counter, thinking this guy might be impressed and move a little quicker if he knew he was dealing with a real live private eye.

"There could be quite a few, so could you be more precise?"

"Yes, I'm looking for any sales or transfers involving Mr. Thomas Sherman and Mr. Dominic Tedesco, both of Hamilton."

At the mention of those names, the man's attitude seemed to shift from going-through-the-motions to paying close attention. And I wondered which name had flipped his switch.

"Have you completed the application form, Sir?"

I could sense the red tape was about to be rolled out. "Not yet."

He riffled through a tray of forms, chose one and placed it on the counter between us. When he moved, those lily pads on his tie seemed to be undulating in a slimy green pond and it was all I could do to keep from grabbing it and pulling tight.

"Unfortunately, by the time you complete the form, it'll be too late for us to search our records because we close at five o'clock."

I glanced at the Register wall clock above the door. "But it's only a quarter to."

I looked around the office; the clerks and secretaries were stowing papers and files in their desks, readying to leave.

"We're open at nine tomorrow. I'll see you then, Mr. –" He checked my card and stuck it in his pocket. "Mr. Dexter."

By the time I got back to my office it was closing time. I heard Trepanier chatting with Isabel and Phyllis as I entered and they seemed to be making arrangements.

"Keep your coat on, Max," Isabel said. "*Robert's* treating us to a drink at the Flamingo Lounge."

I saw the sparkle in the women's eyes, happy, I suppose, because a handsome man had asked them out. Would I be encouraging *Robert* if I agreed to go? Or would I be a horse's ass if I didn't?

I took my coat off and tossed it on a chair. "I'll catch up with you. Got a couple of phone calls to make."

Isabel gave me an inquisitive look but they bustled out and I sat at my desk with no phone calls to make. The Nelligan and Nelligan job would be finished by the end of the week and that would be the last of Trepanier. But would I feel the same way when some other guy became interested in Isabel? I hated to admit that I might've been jealous. No, not might've, damnit, I *was* jealous. So what to do about it? Frank would say, "Be a man, you dumb shit. Tell her how you feel."

I decided the problem was me. How could she really be interested in a small-time private investigator with a two-bit business who was barely making ends meet and limping around like an old man? A guy whose only claim to fame was being awarded the Distinguished Conduct Medal for what the Army called an act of bravery during the Normandy assault. When, in fact, I was stupid enough to think I could save the lives of three guys trapped under rubble and dying when their vehicle was bombed. Instead, two of the men had died and the other had lived but wished he hadn't because he was a quadriplegic. And I nearly lost my own leg in the bargain.

I don't know how long I sat there feeling sorry for myself. It seemed like a long time but was probably less than thirty minutes. I glanced out the window overlooking King Street; it was almost dark, the lights of the city were blinking on and it felt like a different place when night fell and covered up the grubby parts. I pictured Isabel and Phyllis, laughing at *Robert*'s jokes and having a good time at the Flamingo. And I thought, what the hell, and pulled on my coat and grabbed my hat.

CHAPTER TWENTY-SEVEN

I LIMPED WEST ON KING Street and waited with an anxious after-work crowd at the corner of James as a streetcar rounded the corner. The cop finally directed us across and a few doors down I stopped in front of Levinson's Shoe Store. I watched a young guy in the window arranging a display of Hamilton Tiger football stuff which included a life-size mannequin in uniform. I stopped for a moment beside an older man who was directing the guy inside. The mannequin wore Frank Filchock's number and was poised to throw the ball.

"You must be a real football fan," I said to the guy.

"We like to do this every year. It's our Fall tribute to the greatest team in the world."

I turned to face him. "A true believer, eh? You didn't mind that Filchock got booted out of the NFL in that big betting scandal?"

"That was an American thing. We run a clean show here in Hamilton."

That's not what I'd heard. Canadian football teams were offi-cially amateur but it was an open secret that players were paid under the table. In Filchock's case, I'd read that the Tigers paid him seven grand a year as player-coach. Big dough for running after an inflated pigskin, if you asked me. But I didn't want to argue with the guy.

So I crossed over King at MacNab and spotted the Flamingo halfway down the block on the right. Above its entrance hung a ten-foot neon sign winking on and off: a flamingo wearing a top hat and smoking a cigarette in a long holder. A sandwich board sign on the sidewalk announced: **One Nite Only: The Fabulous Ink Spots.**

As I approached the club on the opposite side of the street, I was passing an alley used for deliveries by Robinson's Department Store when two dark figures emerged. I quickened my pace, looking around but seeing no other passersby. One of the guys clamped his hand over my mouth, and together they wrestled me into the darkness of the alleyway as I kicked and struggled to get free. I managed to sink my teeth into the hand on my mouth and that earned me a rap in the ear which set off a ringing in my head.

I got one arm loose and swung it blindly toward the shorter of the two thugs who seemed to be grinning, enjoying his work. Then the guy behind me spun me around and gut-punched me, dropping me to my knees. As I rolled over, I kicked upward, connecting with something soft, and heard an angry growl.

Now a grizzly face was close to mine, a garlicky breath making my eyes smart. "You piece of shit gumshoe, think you're a tough guy, eh?" And he lashed out with a boxer's stinging jab to my right eye, and then another.

They must been following me, because one of them knew exactly which of my knees to step on and apply pressure. I damn near passed out with the electric pain that shot through me.

Garlic-breath was back in my face, saying, "You ain't ever heard of Tedesco, have ya, Gimpy?"

It was harder to see now, my right eye swelling fast, and I thought I might throw up.

The big ape leaned in close, grabbing my lapels, and pulled me toward him, his boxer's face scarred and puffy, close to mine, his voice like a cannon's roar. "Can't hear ya, Gimpy. Speak up."

I tried to shake my head but it made my eyes water. I finally managed to croak, "Never heard of him."

He let me go and my head banged off the stones and gravel in the alley. Before I passed out, I spotted a third man standing in the shadows behind those thugs, smoking a cigarette, passively watching my beating. For a second, before my vision clouded over, I thought it might be Thomas Sherman. But this guy was taller, with sharper features. I didn't have time to ask for his name before I slumped to the ground.

When I came to, I tried to focus on the blurry face close to mine. It was a man, clean-shaven, coffee on his breath. And wearing a cop's uniform. He helped me to sit up, a big arm across my back. "Too much to drink, Pal?"

I shook my head and it hurt like hell so I stopped. I licked my lips, tasted no blood. I opened my mouth and nothing came out on my first attempt. I tried again. "Call Frank Russo. Please."

The cop propped me against the wall and placed a garbage can on either side so I wouldn't topple over. He must have figured me for a friend of Frank's because he said, "Be right back. I'll call it in."

While he was gone, I could hear laughter and voices across the road, revellers coming and going from the Flamingo – where I should have been, instead of staying back at the office wallowing in self-pity. Sometimes I'm such a jerk. I carefully felt my sore eye. And my throbbing knee. Right now I had every right to feel abused and to pity myself. But I didn't. No, I was madder than hell and I wanted to make those bastards pay for sandbagging me.

I probably dozed off because I don't remember Frank arriving. He had me standing up, an arm around me, guiding me to a squad car. "Bad enough for St. Joe's? Or home to my place where Angie can patch you up?"

"Angie." I'd spent more than enough time in hospitals and had no wish to return.

As we drove back to Frank's place, he continued to pump me for details, maybe thinking I wasn't giving him the full story. He knew me too damn well. And I was pushing back; I didn't want to say it was Tedesco's boys because I'd never hear the end of it.

"It was dark, Frank. I didn't recognize either one of them."

"Yeah, but what did they say? You're not gonna tell me it was a robbery, are you?"

My right eye was swollen shut and my knee throbbed like blue blazes. I was in no mood for the third degree and kept my trap shut.

We reached Frank's house on Mulberry Street and he parked at the curb. "C'mon, Maxie, tell me what's goin' on. I can't help you if I don't know what the hell we're talkin' about."

By then he'd worn me down – my will to resist was out the window. I took a couple of deep breaths preparing myself for his reaction. "Tedesco's thugs. They tried to convince me I'd never heard of him."

Frank didn't blow his top as I'd expected. He remained quiet for a moment, then he reached across the seat with one of his big paws and squeezed my arm like a big brother. "You're gonna be okay, Maxie. And try to look on the bright side of this mugging. It shows you've got the Mob's attention – and they're running scared."

I turned to look at him out of my good eye, a teasing grin behind his five o'clock shadow. But at least he wasn't giving me hell for nosing into police business. He knew it wouldn't do any good.

I told him about my visit to the Provincial Building to check on possible land transactions involving the Shermans and Tedesco. "I gave the guy there my card. And I saw him twitch when I said 'Tedesco', so he must've tipped the Mob. But it's hard to believe they'd react that quickly."

"If you don't believe it, just look in the mirror, Bub."

Frank brought me into the house and Angie performed her Florence Nightingale magic on my injuries, fussing over me like a new baby. She'd insisted that I stay over so she could check on me during the night, in case the bleeding around my eye began again. But I turned down their offer to sleep on their living room couch and Frank drove me home.

He parked at the curb and helped me out of his car. Then with an arm around my waist, walked me slowly into my apartment. "Did you have your gun with you?"

"No, I didn't."

"Well, if I were you, I'd dig it out of the mothballs and stick it in your pants."

"Good advice, Frank."

Back in my apartment, I made myself a cup of Mother Parker's Orange Pekoe and brought it into the bedroom with me. I stripped off my dirty clothes; the suit jacket was grease-stained and bloody from the alley and my pants were ripped at the knee. I didn't recognize the guy in the bathroom mirror – he looked like one of those patched-up victims of the Blitz I'd seen in London.

I followed Angie's instructions and made a cold pack for my knee with some ice cubes wrapped in a tea towel, and sank into bed. I was thinking about Frank's remark about carrying my gun. Actually it was my father's; a .32 Colt revolver, a police model from the time he was on the Hamilton force. Frank had gotten me a permit to carry it, signed by the Deputy Police Chief, a friend of his. I wasn't in the habit of taking it with me because I'd never had the occasion to use it. Well, that was about to change.

The incessant jangle of the telephone rescued me from another beating in that alley which I'd been reliving in a nightmare. That memory lingered and I felt again those vicious blows to my head and gut, the pressure on my wounded knee. I wasn't usually a vengeful type of guy but this was different. I limped slowly to the kitchen and glanced at the wall clock, surprised that it wasn't yet midnight, and I braced myself before lifting the receiver. Nobody calls at this time of night with good news.

"Max, it's Isabel. Sorry to call so late but Grace is in trouble. I'll pick you up in 15 minutes if that's okay."

The guy in the bathroom mirror didn't appear to be a helluva lot better than the last time I'd looked. But his five o'clock shadow was much darker. I washed up, got into some clean clothes and waited for Isabel at the entranceway to my apartment. I'd remembered to retrieve my father's revolver from the Stetson hat box where I kept it at the back of my closet. I'd taken the time to clean it, then snugged it into its leather shoulder holster and strapped it on.

As I was waiting I tried to come up with a plausible reason for my bruises and black eye. I watched Isabel's red Studebaker glide to a halt and she rolled down the window to wave at me.

I limped to the curb, slower than usual, stepped into the car and shut the door quickly to extinguish the interior light. If I didn't turn my head toward her when we spoke, I thought she might not notice my shiner. Then I stopped myself. What the hell was I thinking? I couldn't disguise my facial scrapes and bruises, so why was I trying to? Was I really so vain? Was I trying to impress Isabel, show her I was tougher than Humphrey Bogart, some kind of movie hero who laughed at pain? Or, closer to home, braver than *Robert*?

I turned to face her and watched her eyes widen in shock. I reached for her hand and held it tightly. "Take a good look. Scrapes and bruises. And a big black eye."

With her other hand she covered her mouth but waited for me to finish.

"Yes, it hurts like hell but I'll heal. A couple of Tedesco's men worked me over. It tells us we're on the right track, thinking there's a Mob connection to Mr. Sherman's murder."

"Oh, Max. I'm so sorry this happened; just look at you."

I saw tears at the corners of her eyes and shuffled myself closer on the seat. "I'm hurting on the outside, Iz. But I'm mad as hell on the inside. I'm convinced the Mob is trying to get their fingers into the Sherman family business, if they haven't done so already. And it's just so damn unfair that Roger Bruce is paying the price for their greed. That's why we can't quit this case now."

I reached over and touched her tears with my finger. "Now tell me about Grace."

CHAPTER TWENTY-EIGHT

ISABEL COMPOSED HERSELF AND WE drove toward the Sherman house on Park Street to see Grace.

"What time did she call you?"

"About 10:30 or so. I was getting ready for bed. And she was in a real state, Max. Scared out of her wits. Thomas Sherman had come to see her and made a proposition. More like a threat, I'd say. And thank goodness, Vincent was sleeping over at his friend's house down the street and wasn't home to hear their argument."

We were driving west on Hunter Street and she stopped for the traffic light at James South. She turned to face me. "Thomas said he's going to court to overturn his father's will. He's convinced he'll win because he says Grace is in the country illegally —"

"So I guess he doesn't know she's already a Landed Immigrant."

"That's right. And she kept quiet so he's none the wiser. But he also warned her that he'd tell the court she'd duped the old man, gotten him to change his will by sexual favours. Exactly as she'd done with him."

"What? Grace was involved sexually with Thomas? *And* his father? I don't believe it."

"And you'd be right, Max. She says it's a pack of lies. Grace says it was Thomas who made advances to her back when she was a maid in Toronto. When he visited there, Thomas was taken with her right away, a beautiful and exotic Jamaican girl. She wasn't interested, but he … forced himself upon her, made her pregnant with Vincent. But she kept quiet about it because she feared she'd be deported."

The light changed and Isabel drove on.

"Wait a minute. She told us she was married."

"She was. But after Vincent was born. Grace says it's not that unusual in Jamaica for men to marry women with children, whether they were born in wedlock or not. So her husband, who was also from Jamaica, accepted Vincent as his own. When he was killed in the war and she moved to Hamilton, no one else but Thomas knew who the real father was."

"But why would he bring that up in court? He'd be incriminating himself."

"That's what I said, Max. But he's intending to testify that she seduced him in order to legalize her situation. He says, who's going to believe her – a scheming domestic servant – just another one of those shifty Negroes."

"It's probably true that her testimony wouldn't hold up too well against the word of a rich white businessman. So we'll need to dig up some proof that Thomas violated her. Maybe some of Grace's relatives in Toronto could speak on her behalf."

"That's another problem, Max. She won't testify."

Isabel stopped in front of the big house on Park Street and turned to face me, concern etched upon her face.

"Why won't she testify?"

"Because Vincent would learn that his father is actually Thomas, a secret that Grace has vowed to keep. Vincent idolizes Owen; she can't let him find out that Thomas is actually his father. Remember when Grace told us that Thomas was not what he seemed to be? It's so true, Max. He actually tried to bribe Grace; he said he'd give her a nice little pension if she shut up and let his appeal proceed without her opposition. When she said no, he threatened to take her to court for seducing his father so she'd inherit some of his estate. He said she'd be deported too. That snake knows where she's vulnerable and he's taking advantage of it. We have to stop him."

Isabel's face was flushed and her eyes sparkled with passion. She was furious. And she was beautiful.

Grace met us at the door and ushered us in. As usual we sat at the kitchen table, where her eyes flicked from Isabel to me, then remained downcast. This woman was a shadow of the Grace we'd seen before, so full of worry and fear that her eyes barely widened when she saw my mangled face.

"Thanks so much for coming. I can't tell you how much it means to me. We barely know each other, yet here you are in the middle of the night, helping me out."

Isabel moved closer to her and held her hand. "You're a good person, Grace. You'd do the same for us."

I watched Grace wipe a tear from her cheek and level her breathing. "Vincent and I need to get out of here. Maybe we'll take a small apartment somewhere or go to a hotel. I just can't stay in this house – Thomas could return at any time. I'm scared for us. For Vincent."

Isabel said, "Don't be so hasty. I've got plenty of room at my place and that's where we're going. But what about Vincent? Is he okay at his friend's house for tonight or do you want to pick him up now and take him with us?"

Grace exhaled a long breath she'd been holding and her shoulders slumped. "Thank you very much. I'd like to get Vincent right away but it might be too upsetting for him at this hour. So maybe we could get him in the morning."

Isabel stood. "Let's go upstairs and pack. I'll give you a hand."

I watched them mount the stairs; they could have been sisters if you didn't notice their skin colour. Then it occurred to me that Thomas Sherman could easily locate Grace and continue to pressure her. He was working with Tedesco, after all, and finding people was a Mob specialty. But then I thought – when they found Grace, they'd also find Isabel. I was starting to wonder if I was in over my head.

CHAPTER TWENTY-NINE

I WAS LATE FOR WORK the next morning. Again. During the night, Iz and I had taken two large suitcases of clothing for Grace and Vincent from the Sherman house over to her place on Ravenscliffe Avenue, just a few blocks away. When I got back to my apartment it was oh-dark-thirty, if not later, and my knee felt like it was swollen to the size of a pumpkin.

I'd flopped on my bed, didn't bother undressing, and passed out. Some hours later I was awakened by a convention of star-lings which assembled near my bedroom window around 0800 and I lay awake listening to them squabble like bargainers at the Hamilton Market. A half-hour later the Royal Oak delivery guy dropped off a quart of homogenized at my kitchen door. Those damn bottles always rattled like a Gatling gun in their metal carrier.

My mind was filled to overflowing with thoughts of Isabel coming to Grace's rescue, and young Vincent, whom she'd planned to pick up this morning and take back to her place to be with his mother. And Thomas Sherman, that overprivileged swine who'd taken advantage of a vulnerable young Grace then let her find her own way out of her predicament. And now he was back, trying to take advantage of her again.

And I thought about Dominic Tedesco, who made a very nice living by exploiting his victims' soft spots, capitalizing on their greed, then disposing of them when they were no longer useful to him.

And finally, Roger Bruce, who'd found himself in the wrong place at the wrong time: an innocent man who was paying the price for somebody else's sins. Maybe he wasn't a perfect man – it still hurt that he'd lied to me – but, when I thought about it, I didn't know anyone who could lay claim to being perfect. Certainly not me.

The solution seemed simple: untangle the relationship between Thomas Sherman and Tedesco that ultimately resulted in Mr. Sherman's death. Then Roger Bruce would be released from the Barton Street Bastille and justice would prevail for the people of Hamilton. Simple, right?

God, what a dreamer I was. Maybe it was my weakened state, bashed and battered by those street thugs. Or maybe my brain had suffered a direct hit. At 0900 I dragged myself from my bed and under a hot shower until I felt halfway normal.

I finished my second cup of Maxwell House during the sports report on the radio. Vic Copps was saying, "... and the Brooklyn Dodgers' Jackie Robinson received the Rookie of the Year Award. Last year Robinson played for the Montreal Royals and is the first Negro to play in the Major Leagues. You can bet his experience here in Canada went a long way toward his success." Good old Vic – you could always count on him to root for the home team.

And I thought about Jackie Robinson. Now there was a guy with grit and determination like no other. He faced impossible odds yet somehow overcame them. The kind of man I'd like Max Dexter to be.

I phoned for a Veterans Cab to take me to work. No way I could hike from my apartment down to King Street to catch a streetcar. When the car arrived I didn't know the driver; he was probably a temporary, filling in for one of the regulars.

He gave me the once-over as I manoeuvred into the back seat. "Where to, Pal? St. Joe's or the General Hospital?"

I gave him the address of my office and shut up. My entire face ached and I had no desire to chit-chat with this guy. He finally turned around and drove.

As soon as I limped into the lobby of my office building, I almost knocked into my Uncle Scotty.

"Holy shit, Max! That eye looks like a pound of raw hamburger. What did you do to get such a shellacking?"

"I was ambushed, Unc. I think it was a gang of reporters."

He gave his head a vigorous shake, dandruff flying in all directions. Then he grasped the lapel of my jacket and pulled me close. "You're the only nephew I've got, Laddie. You've got to take better care of yourself. Or get a bodyguard."

"You haven't asked me for your daily briefing yet."

He humphed. "Only because you'd give me a load of malarkey again. Tell me what happened to you."

"Sleepwalking. Walked right into the bathroom door and – splat."

"See what I mean? I ask you a simple question and get nothing but bullshit in return."

"I'm sorry, Unc, but I can't say what's going on right now. As soon as I can, you'll be the first to know."

I left him spluttering in the lobby and Tiny took me up to the third floor.

When I entered my office Phyllis and *Robert* had their heads together, no doubt wondering where Max and Isabel were.

Phyllis gasped when she saw my face. "Good Heavens, Max. What in the world happened to you?"

I forced a grin but it hurt like hell; it wasn't easy pretending to be a tough guy, even with a gun under my coat. "I had a disagreement with a couple of guys last night. They won."

Trepanier came closer and examined my face. "You should be home in bed. That's a very big shining."

"Shiner," I said. "A black eye is a shiner."

"However you say, it looks very painful."

I gave them a vague description of the events of last night and the reason for Isabel's temporary absence. "You've got more interviews lined up today?" I asked *Robert* and he nodded his head. "If you need any help just let me know." He wore a quizzical look on his handsome mug, maybe wondering what I wasn't telling him.

I sat at my desk reviewing my case notes. Nothing in them seemed to suggest that I'd be in for a shit-kicking like I got in that alley last night. It was clear that we had to stop Thomas from following through on his threats to Grace, but I was in no shape to go ten rounds with him. As I often did in such circumstances, I called upon my boyhood friend.

When I got him on the phone Frank barked at me. "What the hell's the matter with you? You should be home in bed, you idiot."

"Thanks for your advice, Frank. But there's work to be done. Got time for lunch today?"

I could hear him fuming on the other end of the line. "You take the cake, Buster. What time?"

I'd suggested we meet in my office; that way I wouldn't have to go anywhere where I'd scare the civilians with my bruised-up mug. And I asked Phyllis to pick up some lunch at the White Spot for us.

Frank and I sat at the large table in my office where we ate our 'Spiro's Special' meatball sandwiches, washed down with Cokes.

"You look worse than you did last night, Maxie. That big bruise around your eye looks like an overripe peach. But I know you won't take time off so I won't waste my breath. Now, what were you so anxious to talk about?"

"It's about Thomas Sherman." I filled him in on Thomas's visit to Grace, his threats, and his attempt to bribe her so she wouldn't oppose him in court when he contested his father's will.

"Jeez, he's a mean little bugger, isn't he?"

"He's desperate, Frank. I think he might be in over his head with Tedesco. If he does go to court about the will and fails to win the case, then he won't own the land which I suspect was part of a deal with the Mob. And you know what'll happen to him if he disappoints the Mob boss."

"So now I bet you've got a little job for me."

"Since you offered –"

He gave me his hard cop stare but it wasn't working today. I think he was feeling sorry for his banged-up pal.

"What do you think about hauling Thomas in for questioning? Shake him up and see what comes out. You could tell him you have a witness who saw him with Tedesco, make him sweat a little. And maybe you're suspicious about a certain unnamed guy who made a quick visit to his father's house *after* the guy who's now in jail for his murder. Thomas isn't a man with a strong character, Frank. If you hit him with a few examples about what happened to guys who've run afoul of the Mob, I think you could get him to sing like a canary."

Frank leaned back in his chair and wiped the meatball stain from his tie with a paper napkin. "Any more Cokes?"

I dug into the paper bag on the table and passed him another along with the bottle opener.

He popped the top and took a long swig, then burped. "That feels better."

I remained silent waiting for his mind to process the stuff I'd been feeding him along with the sandwich.

"It's not a bad idea. Let me think about it."

CHAPTER THIRTY

MIDAFTERNOON I WAS STILL AT my desk when the phone rang. I felt good when Frank identified himself and I hoped he'd decided to pick up Thomas Sherman and run him through the hoops.

"Meet me outside your office. It's urgent."

"What's goin' on, Frank? Tell me what's happened."

"Outside your office," he barked in my ear. "Now."

I spotted him at the curb where he'd stopped in front of the Capitol Theatre. I eased into the front seat and slammed the door. "Where are we going?"

"St. Joe's."

"C'mon, Frank. I don't need a hospital; we need to wind up this case with Thomas Sherman and his vicious pals."

He'd just turned left at James and stopped for the traffic light on Main Street. "Isabel's in there."

"What?"

"You heard me. I just got a call from Grace Clarke. Isabel was driving her over to Park Street to pick up her son. They'd just pulled onto Aberdeen when a car muscled its way past them and forced them off the road and into a telephone pole. Other driver took off."

I was shocked – my head was spinning so I hung onto the armrest. Bad enough that I'd got beaten up in that alley. But not Isabel, too. No, no, no. Now my gut stopped churning and a chill came over me, head to toe. I felt a rage building in my chest, ready to burst. Goddamnit! Attacking Isabel was out of bounds. And now I was overcome with that bred-in-the-bone need for vengeance.

Frank nudged me. "You okay?"

"She's alive, right? Tell me she's alive, Frank."

"She's all right. Cuts and bruises. Something about her ankle."

I let out the breath I'd been holding while he spoke. What a relief. She's alive. Cuts and bruises and an ankle weren't life-threatening. Tension slowly ebbed from my limbs and I needed to go to the bathroom.

"What about Grace? Was she hurt, too?"

Frank shook his head. "It scared the hell out of her but she's okay. She picked up Vincent from school and now they're back at Isabel's.

We'd reached the foot of the Mountain, where Frank wheeled into the Emergency entrance at St. Joe's, abandoning the police car where the ambulances parked.

Hustling through the double doors Frank was holding up his police badge and the people in the corridor made way for us as we angled toward the admitting desk.

A nun in a white uniform looked up from a ledger in front of her. 'Sister Rosemary' was etched on her name tag. She glanced at Frank's badge and said, "Yes, Officer?"

"Isabel O'Brien. Car crash. We need to see her right away. Police business."

She looked him over coolly. I figured his pushy urgency was a daily occurrence here and she took it in stride. We followed Sister through a set of swinging doors into the Emergency ward where a row of beds was curtained off. We stopped in front of the third bed along the line and she pulled back the curtain.

Isabel's head rested against a couple of pillows where the bed was elevated. Her red curls were pressed close to her skull and several facial and head cuts were patched with small bandages. Her right leg was exposed from the knee down and rested on a pillow; her ankle was red and swollen and seemed misshapen. She opened her eyes as we approached, and gave us an anemic wave with her fingers which nearly broke my heart. I'd never seen this strong woman so vulnerable and I felt an overwhelming urge to do something, anything to help her get well.

Frank remained at the foot of the bed when I drew nearer and held her hand. "I'm so sorry, Iz. I got you into this and look what happened. It's all my fault."

She tried to speak but her lips were cracked and dry and she just coughed. I picked up the glass of water by the bed and held the straw for her to drink.

"That's better, Max," she spoke in a faint whisper. "How's that eye feeling?"

I had to smile. Laid up in Emergency and she's concerned about my black eye. "I can't see it so it doesn't bother me."

She gave me a weak grin in return and pointed to her ankle. "Doctor says it's broken. They took X-rays and now we're waiting for a specialist."

Frank had moved up beside me, his hat in his hand. "I'm sorry for your injury, Isabel. Are you all right to answer a few questions?"

She opened her eyes a little wider and motioned with her hand for Frank to continue.

He smiled at her. "You and Max make a great pair. The lame and the lamer —"

Isabel pressed her lips together and Frank hurried on. "Do you remember what happened?"

"Black car, a Chev I think, squeezed us off the road on Aberdeen just as I was turning from Ravenscliffe. So I wasn't going that fast." She motioned toward the glass of water and I gave her another sip. "Hit the brakes and slammed into a telephone pole on the driver's side. I felt my ankle bend and crack. I think I must have fainted then."

Frank said, "But it could've been a lot worse. Lucky you only sideswiped that pole."

"Not lucky — a standard defensive manoeuvre. And it was no accident, Frank. That guy meant business."

As he listened, his mouth turned up at the corners then he turned to face me, shaking his head. "Peas in a pod. You're both too smart for your own good."

Isabel managed a hint of a smile and closed her eyes. I moved closer to Frank and lowered my voice. "They've probably given her a shot for the pain. Maybe we should come back later."

We returned to the nurses' station and I caught Sister Rosemary's attention. "When do you expect the doctor to arrive?"

"He should be here soon. There's a waiting room just around the corner. I'll call you."

A dozen or so wooden chairs were jammed into the tiny room next door where two old women in black sat stoically fingering their beads. I picked up a copy of *Liberty* magazine from a low table as we sat down. I flipped through the pages but nothing registered. Thoughts of Isabel filled my mind: the image of her dancing to *The Dipsy Doodle*; the wry smile on her face when she called me 'Boss'; the expert way she drove her Studebaker, with such a light grip on the steering wheel. And now ...

A brisk young guy in a white coat wearing a stethoscope around his neck appeared at the door. "Sister said the police—"

Frank was on his feet, reaching out to shake his hand. "Sergeant Russo. We're with Miss O'Brien. How is she?"

"Nothing we can't fix. But ankle fractures can be tricky. I've seen the X-rays and I'll be consulting with the Chief of Orthopaedic Surgery. We'll operate right away. After that, it's a cast and crutches; you probably know the drill."

I breathed a sigh of relief from my chair and Frank thanked him.

"Leave a phone number," the doctor said. "Sister will call when Miss O'Brien's out of Recovery. Oh, and we've notified her father; he's on our Board of Directors, you see."

Oh, shit. Now I'd have to do another run-in with J. B. O'Brien, a pompous ass who believed he was better equipped to plan Isabel's future than she was.

Frank drove me to my apartment and we sat outside in his car for a few minutes. "When I get back to the office, I'll order up a guard for Isabel's room. Just in case."

"Thanks." Then it struck me. "What the hell does it say about our city, Frank, when an innocent young woman needs a police guard in the hospital just in case the Mob decides to hit her again?"

He thought about my question for a long moment. "Says a helluva lot, doesn't it?"

We sat in silence, tired and worried. Then I said, "You didn't finish telling me about Grace. She's shaken up but not hurt?"

"That's right, just a few bruises. And she's afraid Thomas Sherman had something to do with the crash."

"And what do you think?"

"I'd be surprised if he did. I think the Mob's sending you another message, Bud. Last night's little workout in the alley. Now Isabel's hit and run. You think it's maybe time to back off?"

My taking a beating was one thing – but an attack on Isabel was something else. And Frank knew damn well that I wasn't going to throw in the towel. I leaned across the car seat and punched him on the arm. "Maybe I should report it to the police."

He barked a laugh. "That's an idea. But I understand Mob violence is very difficult for the police to control."

"Yeah, I heard that, too. What would you do? If you were in my shoes?"

He thought about that for a moment. "Just what you're doin' I guess. Hook up with my best friend on the police force and cover my ass as best I could."

CHAPTER THIRTY-ONE

WHEN I ENTERED MY APARTMENT, I dropped my keys in a small brass dish on the table in the hallway and my nostrils twitched. I stood in the doorway between the kitchen and the living room and checked both rooms. I caught a pungent whiff of aftershave lotion, the kind you buy at the five-and-dime for a dollar a gallon.

I followed my nose from the kitchen into my bedroom, a stronger odour in here. One of the dresser drawers was slightly open. I looked inside – my underwear was still there but the white briefs were mixed in with the blue boxers, something I never did. And the closet door was ajar; my two suits and a sports coat were squished together, the pockets of my pants were turned out. The Stetson hat box was on the floor but its former contents were now firmly secured in my shoulder holster.

Someone wanted me to know he'd taken a look around. Looking for …? Since nothing seemed to be missing I decided someone was sending me another message, something to tighten my sphincter. It was working.

I'd spoken with people who'd been burglarized and they claimed it wasn't so much the value of the stuff which was stolen; no, it was the sense of invasion, of personal violation which they'd felt. And now I knew it to be true.

I checked my watch; it was 1800. I limped into the living room and sat in my one comfy chair, feet on the ottoman. What should I do about my intruder? It didn't take me long to realize there was bugger all I could do. Someone was telling me I'm under their microscope. Message received.

Isabel was probably out of surgery by now and I wanted to see her, but I hadn't eaten yet. I called Veterans Taxi and got Lefty again. "Don't you get any time off?" I asked him.

"Yep. I get a half-day on Christmas."

We shared a chuckle before I got down to business. "Is Dave around by any chance?"

"Yeah, he's just about to punch out. Hang on a sec."

In a moment Dave's loud voice boomed over the line. "How ya doin', Max? Are we gonna take a run out to that Burlington golf course again?"

"Not today, Dave. I'm going up to visit someone at St. Joe's and I was thinking we could grab something to eat at the Corktown before you dropped me off at the hospital. Unless you've got something better to do." I needed some kind of normal in this mess, and supper with Dave seemed to fit the bill.

"No, that's fine with me. I'll be right over to pick you up."

After we'd eaten our fish and chips and drunk our Guinness, Dave dumped me at St. Joe's main entrance on John Street and leaned across the seat to shake my hand. "Be careful, Max."

Sister Rosemary was still on duty and she recognized me from this afternoon. That was one benefit of having a memorable black eye. Maybe the only one.

"I can tell you the surgery went very well. She's out of Recovery and in her room now. Second floor, end of the hall. Room 200."

I took the elevator then limped to the end of the hallway where a beefy cop was seated beside the door. I recognized him as a friend of Frank's whom I'd met a couple of times. When he stood I shook his hand. "Good to see you, Murph. I'll rest easier knowing you're here."

I opened the door and stuck my nose in. A big private room. And a window facing the Mountain. And there was J. B. O'Brien sitting beside the bed, reading the newspaper.

When I entered he didn't put down the paper or stand to greet me. Instead he turned toward me and with a stingy nod of his head said, "Dexter."

I ignored him and approached Isabel from the other side of her bed. Her eyes were open but they had a glazed look, probably the result of a sedative. I leaned in close and held her hand. "You're looking much better," I told her.

She gave me a weak smile and pointed to her ankle, which appeared to be glowing in its white plaster cast. Her toes peeked out at the bottom and the cast extended halfway up her calf. She waved me a little closer and spoke in a hoarse whisper. "Now we can limp together."

I smiled as I reached for the glass of water on the side table and held it for her as she took a few sips.

Isabel's father rattled his paper to get my attention. "Fine mess you've gotten my daughter into, Dexter. She even needs a police guard outside her door. I hope you're proud of yourself."

Isabel raised her head and gave him a dark look. "I think it's time for you to go, Dad."

He glared back at her, then at me, and seemed unsure of what to say. He'd harboured a grudge against me since last summer when he was forced to give up an expensive painting which had been looted by Nazis. And it was only his connections with rich associates that had kept him out of jail, because he knew damn well he was in possession of stolen goods. It didn't help that Isabel and I were instrumental in having that painting taken from him. In addition, he was still smouldering because Isabel had left his lucrative accounting firm to join my fledgling detective agency. There were a few reasons why Max Dexter wasn't J. B. O'Brien's favourite person.

He folded his paper and stuck it under his arm as he stood by Iz's bed, gazing at his only child ... "If you need anything ..." Then he turned and marched from the room.

I pulled a chair closer and sat. "He's in fine form this evening."

She made a waving motion with her hand, as if it didn't matter what he did or thought. "I've stopped worrying about him," she said in her hospital voice. "He'll do what he wants to do. He thinks he can buy his way back into my favour with this fancy private room."

"Enough about him. How does your ankle feel?"

She gave her head a tiny shake. "It throbs a bit but they're giving me painkillers."

"Good. When will they let you out?"

"Probably tomorrow. It's just a matter of healing now. This cast for six weeks then a walking cast. It could have been so much worse, Max."

I was squeezing her hand now, my head close to hers. "When Frank told me about the crash, I thought I might've lost you. You're such a big part of my life now, I just don't know what I would've done if..."

"Don't worry so much, Max. I'm going to be fine. And we'll be going to the Circus Roof again soon. I promise."

I leaned even closer and our lips brushed together. When I pulled back I could feel my heart thumping in my chest.

Those lips were smiling at me now. "That was a long time coming, Max. But worth the wait."

I felt a pleasant buzzing in my limbs, a tingling electrical charge. And my mind was racing, thinking of what to say. Or maybe, for a change, I should keep my foot out of my mouth. I'd never quite felt like this before. Then a strong force took hold of me and I drew closer and we kissed again. A little longer this time. And after a moment, I sat back in my chair, feeling like a kid in Gus's Confectionery with a five-cent bag of jujubes and a pair of wax lips.

Isabel's face had a rosy glow, the spray of freckles across her nose and cheeks less visible now. But that blush soon ebbed away, replaced by a wary frown as she squeezed my hand, hard. "I'm still frightened, Max, for both of us. Looking at you, your face so battered I want to cry. And with this cast on there's little I can do to help. Who are these people? Will they go after Grace and Vincent next?"

I shared her feeling of helplessness. And I felt a gangster's grip tightening around my throat, making my voice come out in a croak. "We're doing what we can, Iz. And I know it doesn't seem like enough. But Frank's on the job and there's a guard at your door. You're right to be worried about Grace and her son. I'll ask Frank to have a patrol car checking your place."

"But why is this happening to us, Max? We don't even know these people."

I shook my head; it was difficult to express evil in words. "It's the way the Mob works. Through fear and intimidation.

174 | Chris Laing

They see us as trespassers – snooping into their business, and they intend to put a stop to it – pure and simple. So they'll keep increasing the pressure 'til they get what they want. You're right to be scared, Iz, and so am I."

Then silence settled between us as we held hands and huddled together, like two survivors adrift on a raft, in search of a safe harbour.

"I should let you rest now," I whispered. "I'll see you in the morning."

As I backed toward the doorway, I banged my head against the wall with a thud. She gave a tiny shake of her head and sent me a brave little smile.

CHAPTER THIRTY-TWO

I LEFT ISABEL'S ROOM AND took the elevator down to the main lobby, where I phoned Frank at home.

"I've been trying to reach you," he said.

"Then it must be mental telepathy. What's happening?"

"I've got a date tonight and I thought you might like to come along."

"A date."

"Yeah. Thomas Sherman called the station, asking for the detective investigating his father's death. Said it was urgent. So I got the call at home."

"Confession time, Frank?"

"We'll see. I'm going to his place rather than having him come to the station. He might be more talkative in his home setting."

"Isn't that a job for the Burlington cops?"

"No problem. I called the duty sergeant there, told him I was coming out as part of an investigation. Cops don't like to get involved if they don't have to. Who needs the extra workload, eh?"

"Sure, Frank, I'd like to come along."

"Good. Tell me where you are, I'll pick you up."

Frank arrived at the front entrance of St. Joe's in an unmarked Ford. I checked my Bulova; it was 20:45 and I felt a chill in the air as I limped to his car.

"How's Isabel?" he asked as soon as I slid onto the front seat beside him.

"Pretty frightened. But she's got a lot of spunk. She'll get through this."

He reached across my body and tugged my right arm, turning me so he could see my face. "That's one helluva shiner. How're you doing?"

"I'd be lying if I didn't admit to being frightened, too."

"A normal reaction. Don't be ashamed of it. And I see by the bulge in your jacket that you're finally armed. I'm glad you're watching out for yourself."

His face was half in shadow but I could still make out the spark of determination in his eyes. "We're gonna get to the bottom of this, Max."

He drove west to Dundurn Street then over to York where we crossed over the High Level Bridge. "How come you're taking me with you on a police call, Frank? You're usually such a horse's ass about drawing the line between official business and those 'nosy civilians', as you like to call us."

He grunted as he thought about his reply. "We're in a different situation here. You're my best friend – from childhood for Chrissake. And you just got the shit kicked out of you. Then your assistant, your girlfriend, whatever you want to call her, gets run off the road and she could've been killed. We both know this is how the Mob operates and I've got a feeling that Thomas Sherman could help us build a case against them. If my boss or even the Chief gives me hell for bringing you with me, I don't care. We need to act fast and you can help. And there's no doubt in my mind that you've earned the right to be here."

I swallowed the lump in my throat – I was touched by his little speech. And it felt good that he'd reaffirmed the brotherly feeling we'd always had for each other, cop procedures aside.

"Besides," he flashed me a grin. "I need to keep an eye on you in case you decide to attack another Mob guy."

We drove along Plains Road past Holy Sepulchre Cemetery then he cut down to North Shore Boulevard. I was telling him about Thomas Sherman's meeting with Grace; his threat to go to court to have the new will overturned so he'd inherit his father's entire estate.

"But worst of all for Grace, he said he'd reveal Vincent's paternity in court and blame her for seducing him. Grace says she'd refuse to testify on her own behalf because she'd never allow Vincent to learn that Thomas was his father."

Frank shook his head, "Pretty damn complicated, isn't it?"

I was looking out the window now, trying to read the house numbers in the semi-darkness. "Slow down a bit. It's just past the golf course on the right. Number 492."

We drove up the long circular drive, the car's headlights revealing the sweep of the manicured lawns, the modern design of the huge fieldstone bungalow and, off to the left, the big boat-house on the edge of the bay.

Frank puckered up and blew a low whistle. "Jeez. What a joint, eh?"

We got out of the car and looked around. No other cars were evident and I figured Thomas's must be in the garage. A few lights were on in the house and Frank stepped forward to ring the doorbell.

The guy who opened the door looked nothing like the slick, rich guy I'd met on my last visit here. His clothes looked slept-in, his hair dishevelled and a two-day stubble bristled on his chin. He looked surprised to see me, then did a double take when he noticed my beat-up face. He gathered himself and turned to Frank. "You're Sergeant Russo?"

Frank stuck out his hand and Thomas shook it. "Come in. Come in. You, too, Dexter."

I was surprised he'd remembered my name. But I supposed that's how Thomas and the high and mighty crowd behaved. Even though I might've been the last guy in the world he'd wanted to see, he'd shake my hand, invite me in and offer me a drink.

And sure enough, Thomas pointed to a grouping of leather chairs. "Have a seat. How about a drink?"

When Thomas was pouring drinks at the bar, Frank caught my attention and rolled his eyes at the plush layout in here.

Frank and I had asked for Cokes. Thomas poured himself a healthy belt of whisky and joined us.

"I called the Chief of Police," Thomas said. "And he referred me to you, Sergeant." He shifted in his chair and crossed his legs. Despite his unkempt appearance, he was collected and composed. "I seem to have a little problem."

I was flabbergasted. The guy's world is falling apart; his father's been murdered, but before dying he changed his will, leaving his land holdings to the Anglican Church. That same land which I'd bet Thomas was dealing to Tedesco and company. And now that Thomas can't deliver he says he seems to have a "little" problem. Were all rich guys this stupid?

Frank was the model of patience. He sipped his Coke then set his glass down on the coffee table. "What seems to be the problem, Mr. Sherman?"

"Well, you know how the business world operates – the markets are cyclical, you always have your ups and downs. And most businessmen understand that pattern. I say most, because there are a few who refuse to acknowledge that simple fact. For example, right now I've negotiated a deal with someone who won't accept that I'm experiencing a temporary setback. That person is someone whom I've recently met and it's come to my attention that he's known to the police."

"Interesting," Frank said. "Who is this person?"

"His name is Dominic Tedesco."

Frank gave him his wide-eyed look. "My, my. Dominic Tedesco. How exactly did you become acquainted with him?"

"Through one of my business contacts, who happens to be Mr. Tedesco's lawyer. My father, and now my father's estate, owns a large tract of land which Mr. Tedesco had arranged to buy. But because my father's will ... unexpectedly ... specified that the land would go to the Anglican Church, I'm unable to complete our end of the contract. As a result, Mr. Tedesco is quite upset. And he's threatened me."

Frank was rubbing his chin, apparently considering Thomas's dilemma. "What kind of threat?"

"He said I could meet the same fate as my father."

The room went quiet for a long moment. I was imagining Tedesco delivering that line and a shiver ran up my spine.

Frank said, "You mean he actually admitted to killing your father?"

"Well, not exactly, not in so many words. I thought my father was killed by that artist – the friend of Dexter here." He waved a hand in my direction. "In fact, Dexter came to see me a few days ago and we talked about that."

"But you didn't mention you were doing business with Dominic Tedesco," I said.

He ignored my comment and turned back to Frank. "I'm not naïve, Sergeant. I did know that Mr. Tedesco has an unsavoury reputation. But he seemed honest and above board in all my dealings with him. That is, until he threatened me. So, what do you propose to do about it?"

Frank leaned forward in his chair now and gave Thomas the full force of his hard cop stare. "I propose that you knew a helluva lot more about Tedesco besides his *unsavoury* reputation. That you knew damn well that he'd arranged your father's death. And now I'm wondering if you were his willing accomplice."

Thomas sat back with a thud, as though he'd been punched in the chest. "No goddamn way," he was sputtering now. "You can't prove any of that."

Frank stretched his legs out and leaned back in his chair, still staring at the dishevelled Thomas, now appearing to wilt before our eyes. "Take your time, Mr. Sherman. We've got all night."

Thomas turned to me, panic in his eyes, looking for someone to throw him a lifeline. He opened his mouth and I cut him off. "Grace Clarke told us you'd threatened her. That you planned to contest your father's will and expose the circumstances of her son's birth. Then you tried to buy her off – a nice little pension so she wouldn't oppose your attempt to overturn the will."

He sprang forward in his chair. "That's a damn lie. Don't let her fool you. She's an evil bitch – she weaseled her way into my father's life, promising him sexual favours in hopes of getting her hands on his money. It wouldn't surprise me if she was in cahoots with that artist fellow. Maybe paid him off to kill the old man."

I was about to lay into him when Frank reached over and squeezed my arm to shut me up. He turned back to Thomas. "That's bullshit, Mr. Sherman, and you know it. Now tell us how Tedesco threatened you."

I glanced at Thomas slumped in his chair and was reminded of a newspaper photo I'd seen of the boxer, Billy Conn, whipped and beaten by Joe Louis in their World Championship fight last year. He reached for his drink and finished it in one long gulp, gaining a little false courage. He turned toward Frank but his eyes remained downcast. "He said I'd join my father in Hamilton Cemetery if I didn't get the land."

Frank let that simmer.

Finally, Thomas cleared his throat. "He said I had a week to come up with the land. I tried to convince him I could have the will overturned in court but he wouldn't wait that long. I was frantic; I didn't know what to do. I thought the police could help me."

"Are you willing to testify against Tedesco? Explain to the court how you made a deal with the devil, then couldn't deliver on your part of the bargain? That he threatened to kill you just as he had your father killed?"

"Are you out of your mind? I can't testify against these people – they're too dangerous. I'm a taxpaying citizen and I thought the police would offer me some kind of protection against this man."

Frank drew in a deep breath and exhaled as if he were the long-suffering school principal eyeing the kid holding a cheat sheet and claiming he 'didn't do nuthin' wrong'. "You conspired with Tedesco to sell him your land so he could build apartments or offices, whatever. It didn't occur to you that's how he launders his money? Other taxpaying citizens might wonder why the hell we'd want to protect you, wouldn't they? And if we can't explain that we gave you help in exchange for your testimony, well, we'd be run out of town, wouldn't we?"

I kept my trap shut and watched Thomas fighting with himself. If you asked me, I'd say he was buggered whatever he chose to do. Any way you looked at it, he'd have to pay for his greed.

Frank finished his Coke and stood up. "I'll call you in the morning, Mr. Sherman. You can let me know then what you decide."

CHAPTER THIRTY-THREE

A STIFF NORTH WIND BUFFETED the car as we headed home.

"That was some date, Frank. What d'you think he'll decide?"

"Dunno. I just hope he gets what he deserves. But that ain't always the case with these rich guys, is it?"

We were driving along Plains Road and he pointed to the Rendezvous restaurant. "How about a piece of their apple pie, Max?

"Why not?"

He wheeled into the parking lot and we stopped beside a couple of hot rods, which you were seeing more frequently these days. These were Model A Fords, painted a garish red, customized and souped-up. The Rendezvous was a popular joint; in the evenings it was a hangout for teenagers and college kids. But the food was good and the service fast. We joined the lineup inside and ordered our pie and coffee.

We sat a good distance from the jukebox where some dope had paid a nickel to hear Arthur Godfrey sing *The Too Fat Polka*.

Frank shook his head. "I wonder who told that guy he could sing?"

We watched the kids flirting and joking with each other as we ate. Nobody got up to dance the polka.

Frank ordered his pie à la mode and was now using his spoon to scoop up what remained of his melted ice cream. Then he pushed his plate toward the centre of the table and slid his coffee cup closer. "So you and Isabel." He leaned toward me, his look demanding a straight answer.

"I like her a lot."

"I think it's more than that."

"Well, it's complicated. She's from a far different world than you and I knew on Napier Street. Private school, university degree, more money than Midas. And she's a beautiful woman who could have her pick of the crop. So I ask myself, why the hell would she be interested in me?"

His steady gaze pinned me in my seat and wouldn't let go. "I've always said it, Max."

"Said what?"

"You're a horse's ass when it comes to women."

I didn't respond.

And he didn't let up. "Sure she's rich – and educated – and beautiful. But what does she do? She comes to work with you every day of the week. Shit, she practically runs that office of yours. And I hear you go out on dates. Dancing at the Circus Roof, no less."

"Who told you that?"

He smirked. "A little bird."

I thought about what he said and I had to admit it – I sometimes dared to dream about a future with her. Especially this evening at the hospital when we'd actually kissed. But what if I tried to take it further and she didn't …

"Horse's ass," Frank said again.

CHAPTER THIRTY-FOUR

I don't know how many times I awoke during the night; my knee throbbed, the right side of my face ached and my brain was working overtime. When I began to doze off the image of Isabel crashing into that telephone pole would jar me awake. I pictured her in her hospital bed, foot in a cast. Her pale, frightened face. And I couldn't escape the fact that I was responsible for getting her into this mess.

Small wonder that I'd slept in again this morning. When I arrived at the office it was 0930 and *Robert* had his coat on, ready to leave. "I will finish the interviews today," he said. "Then I go back to my regular job."

I gave him a soft pat on the back. "You've helped us a lot, Bud. We were lucky to have you, even if it was only for a week."

After he left, Phyllis poured a cup of White Spot coffee into a mug and followed me into my office, where she set it on my desk. "*Voilà* Max. Your *café*."

I nodded my thanks. "It's beginning to feel like Paris around here."

She held her skirt with both hands to keep it from creasing as she sat in the chair beside my desk. "How's Isabel doing? I just feel sick about what happened to her."

"Doing a lot better. I saw her last night, a big plaster cast on her foot, but she still has a smile on her face."

"She's such a brave lady, Max. And smart. I'm learning a lot from her."

I smiled at Phyllis; her heart was in the right place. "Why don't you leave a bit early today and visit her? She'd love to see you."

Phyllis lit up like a Christmas tree. "Gee, thanks, Max."

The phone rang and she hustled to her desk to answer it. She buzzed the call through to me.

"Max, it's Marge. From Mr. Sherman's office? I've got a favour to ask."

"You sound a little panicky, Marge."

"Well, I'm concerned, yes. Mr. Sherman left me a note. He said he had a meeting at his office this morning. You know, in the Lister Block. And when I tried to call him there about his other appointments, well, I couldn't get through. So I called the operator and she said the phone's off the hook. Maybe you think I'm just being silly, Max, but I'm worried about him. He just hasn't seemed himself lately. I wondered if you could go over to check on him. I remembered you told me your office wasn't too far away. I really would appreciate it."

A meeting at his downtown office. First thing in the morning. That didn't ring any alarm bells for me but she knew him a helluva lot better than I did. "It's no trouble, Marge, I have to go up that way anyhow," I lied. "I'll drop in and call you back."

I put my coat on and grabbed my fedora. "I won't be too long, Phyllis. Just going over to the Lister Block for a few minutes."

Foot traffic was lighter this morning because of the off-and-on rain showers. I limped up to John Street, one block north to King William, then two blocks west to James Street North where the Lister Block was on the corner. I checked the directory board and found Sherman's office on the third floor so I took the elevator, one of those new-fangled self-operated jobs which put the operators out of work.

When I stepped out of the elevator I followed the arrow to the right. The door had a frosted glass panel lettered *Sherman Investments*. It was unlocked so I entered into a reception area with a secretarial desk. I closed the door quietly behind me. In the waiting area a half-dozen wooden chairs were grouped around a low matching table where a few magazines were neatly piled. I noticed the top one – *Investors Monthly*. I stepped behind what I assumed was Marge's desk – neat and orderly, a couple of filing folders sat in the centre of the green desk blotter. On a narrow shelf was a potted begonia in need of watering, its leaves beginning to brown. I opened the desk drawer – pencils, erasers, paper clips and a roll of Life Savers – Wint-O-Green flavour.

Nothing appeared to be disturbed here and I wondered if Marge was just a well-intentioned worrywart. I crossed the room to a second door which I presumed was the office of the Big Cheese.

I knocked lightly and waited – no response and the eerie silence in here gave me an uneasy feeling. I turned the knob and the door opened. Odd that both doors were unlocked and nobody seemed to be here. The door swung back with a swishing sound as it passed over the pile carpeting. To the left I saw a three-drawer filing cabinet, its bottom drawer pulled out, some documents scattered on the floor. My eyes darted about the room, trying to locate the source of the beeping sound that I thought had come from the street. Then I recalled Marge saying the operator told her the phone was off the hook: I spotted it now as the source of the beeping. And there was Thomas at his desk, his upper body slumped across its surface. His head was facing the window onto James Street where the traffic flowed by in a steady stream, and he still clutched the telephone receiver in his left hand. I shuffled a few steps closer, avoiding the glare from the window and noticed a closet in the corner, its door ajar, the sleeve of a carefully hung overcoat just visible. I turned to the desk, gaping at the pool of blood where Thomas's head rested on the desktop, his throat slit open like a slaughtered animal. His eyes were glazed but seemed to be staring at the trail of blood leading to the edge of the desk where it stopped. I touched his throat; it still felt warm. Then I moved a bit closer, my eyes following that bloody trail onto the floor.

After a gut-wrenching moment I swallowed quickly, fighting the nausea that threatened to overcome me. That's when I heard a faint rustling sound behind me and, acting on reflex, I dropped to my knees, crawling behind the side of the desk.

When I peeked over the edge of the desk I looked directly into Thomas's still-open eyes and a sharp jolt shot through me. I raised my head a little higher and saw a dark figure standing in the closet across the room. The image of the guy in the shadows while I was beaten up in that alley flashed through my mind. I slipped my right hand inside my jacket and removed my revolver.

Now the closet door swung all the way open and a well-dressed man about the size of Thomas Sherman took a step forward and stopped, the desk between us about ten feet in front of him. The same guy I saw driving Tedesco when he'd visited Thomas in Burlington. He wore a tailored dark suit, white shirt and tie, and looked like he belonged in one of these Lister Block offices. Except for the snub-nosed revolver pointing down at me.

"Couldn't keep your nose out of our business, eh, Mr. Gumshoe? I thought you got the message in that alley."

"Some guys are slow learners."

His lips twitched into a grim smile. "There's a remedy for that."

I saw his gun begin to move and ducked my head behind the desk before the echo of two shots filled the room. I rolled quickly to my left, sliding through the slick pool of Thomas's blood on the floor, and got off two shots of my own as the gangster lurched toward me. He fell forward, smacking his head on the far edge of the desk. Blood spurted from that gash as well as the two holes which now bloomed on the front of his white shirt.

I crept toward him as he lay on his back, staring at the ceiling, seeing nothing. I got to my knees and holstered my gun, my hand starting to shake. It wasn't every day that you shot a man to death. Even in the war I'd only had to use my sidearm twice – killing two Jerries who'd managed to slip behind our defences. But this was different ... and if I hadn't shot him ...

I got to my feet and brushed myself off; Thomas's blood stains remained on my suit, sickeningly wet. I limped to the outer office where I intended to use Marge's phone to call Frank Russo but I caught myself in time. I didn't want to leave my fingerprints all over the crime scene.

I left the deafening silence of the office and staggered into the hallway. The bell announcing the arrival of the elevator was earsplitting. I stepped inside and pressed the button for the ground floor.

My hand was still shaking and it took me two tries to insert a nickel in the coin slot of the public phone in the lobby to get

Frank on the line. "I'm at Sherman's office in the Lister Block, third floor. And it looks like someone's made Thomas's decision for him. So you'd better bring the coroner. Tell him we've got two bodies here. One of Tedesco's thugs decided to stay behind."

EPILOGUE

EIGHT DAYS LATER, I TOOK a Veterans Cab to Isabel's home on
Ravenscliffe Avenue, a private paradise off Aberdeen where the
swanks lived, tucked up at the foot of the Mountain away from
all the hurly-burly of the city. I stood in her driveway, admiring
the luxurious homes around me. Her place was a comfortable
two-storey brick building in the Tudor style, one of two homes
on her father's estate before he moved to Ancaster. He'd severed
this piece of property and given it to Isabel when she joined her
father's accounting firm.

In the midst of all this ritziness I was assailed once again
with those nagging doubts about Isabel and how she felt about
me. More than once she'd told me her money was merely part
of the baggage she was born with. Some baggage, I thought, as
I gawked around me. But maybe her perspective was the right
way to see things. She had the ability to look beyond her wealth;
she didn't let it control her life. And in that moment I decided I'd
have to follow her example.

Grace Clarke answered the door. When she grasped my
hand in both of hers I caught a glimpse of the watch on her left
wrist. I did a double take – it looked like that Hamilton watch
from James Jewellers.

"Hello, Max. I want to thank you for everything you've done
for Vincent and me. I'm very grateful."

"I didn't really do that much. Thomas set the wheels in
motion and we just followed him as he brought about his own
fate."

She thought about that a moment and seemed to concur that
Thomas had indeed engineered his own demise. Then she hung
my hat and coat in the hall closet and touched my arm, drawing

closer. "I'm pleased with the way you spoke to Vincent about smoking in those bushes. It wasn't easy for him to tell me about it and I'm proud of my boy."

"He's a great kid, Grace."

I walked behind her into the living room where Iz was propped up by pillows on a long couch by a window facing the rear garden. Her leg rested on an ottoman and I noted the signatures scrawled on her cast. She patted the cushion beside her, waving me over.

"You're looking better every day," I said as I gave her a peck on the cheek. I glanced toward her cast. "I see your autograph book is filling up."

"I can't wait to get it off, Max." She laid a hand on her crutches. "In the meantime I look like Long John Silver using these things."

When Grace returned she fussed with the pillow under Isabel's leg until Iz held her arm. "I'm fine, Grace. You're spoiling me with all your attention."

I pointed to Grace's wrist. "I couldn't help noticing your beautiful watch when we shook hands at the door."

Her eyes flashed from me to Isabel then she bowed her head, staring at her watch. "I didn't admit it was mine when you asked me about it before. I was afraid you'd think I was involved in Mr. Sherman's death."

"We didn't know what to think," Isabel said. "But I know you were only trying to protect your family. And you didn't know us well enough to trust us."

Grace's eyes remained downcast, her right hand touching her watch. "He gave it to me last year. For my birthday." She looked up again and held my eyes. "There was nothing ... physical between us. He was a lonely man. After his heart attack, I looked after him until he got back on his feet. We were friends. He gave me this watch in gratitude."

Isabel extended her arm and Grace looked up, taking her hand. "What about Thomas?" Iz said.

"Thomas was taking the business in a direction Charles didn't approve of. He said his father was old-fashioned, didn't know how to run a business anymore. And now we know what he was really doing with that ... mobster. His father would have been ashamed of him. I can't say I'm sorry about his death."

Isabel leaned back. "Well, it's all over now, Grace. And you're welcome to stay here until you decide about your future."

Grace stood, giving Isabel a warm smile. "Thank you. I'll say good night now. Howard is staying over tonight and the boys are listening to the hockey game on the radio. If it's a close one, maybe I'll sit with them."

We listened to her go upstairs, then the muffled sounds of doors opening and closing.

I moved a little closer to Iz. "How long do you think Grace and Vincent will be staying with you?"

"Well, I'll be getting this cast off in the next few weeks but I couldn't get along without her until then. After that, I'll be a lot more mobile with a walking cast. But I love having them here. It's like having a family, I guess."

She looked away, smiling obliquely. My mind skipped forward in a dream-like vision: I saw myself standing at Isabel's side, my arm around her shoulders, admiring the sweet face of the baby girl cuddled in her arms. I was stroking the child's silky red hair as I gazed into her bright green eyes. Holy Moley, that image scared the hell out of me. Was that really me in the picture?

I pushed the vision away. No point getting ahead of myself.

Our eyes locked as we sat there quietly, I guess what you'd call a pregnant pause. She leaned in closer, her voice quiet. "You know, Max, I've been thinking ..."

A tingle ran up my spine and it settled in my scalp as I held my breath.

"Just look at us. Here I am in a cast and crutches. And you've been beaten and bruised, probably worse than me. And I can't stop thinking about the shootout between you and that gangster. It could have been you who'd been shot and killed, Max. I get the shivers even thinking about it."

I squeezed her hand tightly. "It was just bad luck that he was still there. He heard me in the outer office and hid himself in Thomas's closet. Then when I discovered the body, he knew I'd call the police. I guess he felt he had no choice. He meant to kill me so I had to defend myself."

She pulled me closer, slipping her arm around my neck. "I know that, Max. But I'm afraid of losing you. If we're going to have a future, do you think we should take a closer look at what's important to us?"

Hell's Bells. That caught me by surprise. I thought things were just getting interesting.

END

ACKNOWLEDGEMENTS

ONCE AGAIN I'M GRATEFUL for the work of the Seraphim team: to publisher Maureen Whyte for her ongoing support of my work. And to editor George Down, a thoughtful man who's cornered the market on tact. Thanks to Trudi Down for her marketing and promotional efforts. And to Julie McNeill for her snazzy design of this book.

Special thanks to Catherine London who's a loyal friend of Max and Isabel. I value her editorial advice during all their escapades.

I'm still a big fan of Margaret Houghton's books about Hamilton's history, vanished or otherwise.

Thanks to Pat O'Neill, former governor of the Barton Street Jail, for his still vivid memories of the old place.

I'm also grateful to Jim Suenaga for sharing his first-hand experience of the internment of Canadians of Japanese descent during WWII.

It was a lucky day for me when I met Rod and Lis Latner after the publication of *A Private Man*. Both retired from the Hamilton Police Service, they now work full-time providing me with invaluable bits of Hamilton "stuff".

To my family and friends who recognize their names on some of my characters – it's all in fun, eh?

Finally, thank you to my first and last reader and favourite artist, my wife Michèle LaRose, who will always be my Isabel.

Chris Laing is a native of Hamilton, Ontario. He worked in private business for 20 years before joining the Federal Public Service, where he served in the Department of the Secretary of State and National Museums of Canada until his retirement.

In the past number of years he has expanded his long-time interest in detective stories from that of avid reader to writing in this genre. His short stories have appeared in *Alfred Hitchcock's Mystery Magazine* and *Hammered Out* as well as a number of online journals. His collection of short stories about growing up in Hamilton during World War II, *West End Kid: Tales from the Forties*, was published in 2013 through Smashwords and is available as an e-book from online retailers.

His first novel, *A Private Man*, was published by Seraphim Editions in 2012 and was a Finalist for the Arthur Ellis Award – Best First Crime Novel in 2013 and a Hamilton Arts Council Literary Award.

A Deadly Venture is the second novel in the Max Dexter Mystery Series.

Chris now lives in Kingston, Ontario with his wife, artist Michèle LaRose.